What...
if not
I.I.T.?

"Doors are always open"

What... if not I.I.T.?

"Doors are always open"

Suhail Abidi

Srishti
Publishers & Distributors

Srishti Publishers & Distributors
N-16, C. R. Park
New Delhi 110 019
srishtipublishers@gmail.com

First published by
Srishti Publishers & Distributors in 2012

All characters in this book are fictitous, and any resemblance to real persons, living or dead, is coincidental.

Typeset by EGP at Srishti

Printed and bound in India

PREFACE

I was lying on my bed and my father, full of excitement, entered my room. I was offered admission to Indian Institute of Management Calcutta for their PGP – PGDM (commonly known as MBA) programme.

'Don't come near me.' The reason behind this warning was my condition. I was suffering from a highly contagious viral disease, commonly known as chicken pox. The infection was at its peak due to improper and negligent treatment.

'It's alright, I am immune to this, but promise me beta this time you will join.' He used "this time" because a year back I had refused a similar offer from IIM Lucknow.

'Dad, you know I won't. This is exactly why I wasn't willing to write the CAT exam.'

'But, what is wrong with you. People are dying to get admission in IIMs.'

Three days later.

I was lying on my bed and my mother, sad and depressed, entered my room. One boy in my society, Sankalp, tried to commit suicide, jumping off the terrace, because he could not get through Indian Institute of Technology, Joint Entrance Examination, IITJEE.

'They say he will stay in the hospital for the next few weeks,' she said with tears in her eyes.

I looked at her and tried to show some empathy, while, at the same time, gesturing her to stay away from me. But she came and sat next to me.

'Beta, they say IIM Calcutta is very good.' I looked at her and she without saying anything else started readjusting the huge pile of neem leaves around me.

I was on the same bed for the next 25 days, which made the rest period a total of 45 days. All this time I was thinking as to why students, parents and the society as a whole attach so much importance to a few educational institutes in the country.

After the long siege I was finally able to come out of my room. Sankalp also returned home from the hospital. We went to see him.

What happened in the next two days was a life changing experience, not only for me, but also for a few more people.

Disclaimer:
All characters in this book are totally fictitious, BUT, any resemblance to any person living or dead is purely intentional.

FOREWARD

I was in no mood of taking possession of a seemingly bulk manuscript of this book. That was almost forcibly handed over to me by Suhail's father who has been a close friend, colleague and a younger brother (three in one) for more than a decade now. He had acquired this right as a result of this close association and I had no option. It was in the evening and I was to leave for Delhi by Lucknow Mail. My luggage had already been packed and any addition warranted the engagement of a coolie, which I always like to avoid (they always try to disturb your peace of mind irrespective of your generosity). So I decided to give a little more exercise to my muscles and adjusted the same in my two piece luggage. I opened it in Delhi during my car journey from the place of stay to the place of meeting the next morning.

This was the beginning of the script reading. I knew Suhail as a brilliant son of his father with a strong will-power. He had graduated from IIT Kanpur and easily qualified for admission in IIMs. It was at this point that his will-power became visible. He decided not to join any of them and took his own path. Therefore my curiousity about what he was trying to say in his maiden effort of writing was natural. But the curiosity soon turned in interest and eventually in joy as I started turning the pages. The result was that I completed it in almost one go.

In this book, Suhail is addressing to the dilemma of a large number of young students for whom the definition of success has become a mystery. The traditions of the society, competition with the peer group and the ambitions of parents have made their route of success so narrow, that all the freedom and joy of youth are lost for them. In a competitive society of today, behind one success there are many failures and it is more so in an examination like JEE. Suhail has very carefully and correctly tracked the success stories of those who failed to clear JEE for one reason or the other. Through this book, he is trying to say that there are many doors to success and closure of one does not mean that the others are not open. And he has been greatly successful in establishing his point.

While this message is being given by Suhail in the background of IIT, it holds good in all aspects of life. The life does not end with one examination only. In fact after the life of examination is over the examination of life begins. And this examination is generally more difficult. If attitude of positivity is developed in the beginning itself, success is assured all through the life. According to me there is no competition in success and each of us has a fundamental right on success. The secret is that one can not afford to do less than his or her best. In this book it has been rightly mentioned somewhere that:

"You get what you want; You just have to want it enough".

A few words about the style and language of the book are essential. I have liked both of them and I wonder how Suhail acquired both. His father told me that he has been a voracious reader and improved his vocabulary with a decisive mind. No wonder this is reflected in the book. I think the language is rich and lucid. Moreover, a silent wit runs through the entire book. I congratulate the author (Suhail deserves to be called so) for this successful effort. I am sure the book will go a long way in achieving the desired objective. I also wish many such works from Suhail's pen.

I congratulate the readers also to have chosen this book for reading.

R.K. Mittal*, I.A.S.

*Mr. R.K.Mittal has written over 20 self-help books

ACKNOWLEDGEMENTS

If I start thanking in the order of appearance then the first in line would be Varicella zoster virus (VZV) that infected me with chicken pox which eventually led to the idea of jotting down my thoughts. Second, but equally important is Dr. Agnihotri whose carefree attitude and minor slips miraculously turned my 14 day illness into a 45 day bed rest fiesta with neem leaves on my side.

Thanks to Amita for inspiring me to convert random scribbling into a book.

Ankit: for reading the book 134 times and for being there with me (until he joined IIM Ahmedabad and became mean) and with the book (forever as a character).

Faisal & Bilal: for giving infinite inputs and some real life experiences along with their copyright.

Mamma & Samhita & Shalini: for being exceptionally critical about everything in the book.

Ilmi and RB: for their insightful reviews.

RK Mittal Uncle: for continuous support and guidance.

Last but not the least, Sonu: for refreshing me with his excellent coffee every time I needed it.

1

AND SO IT STARTED

"I'm a great believer in luck, and I find the harder I work the more I have of it"

-Thomas Jefferson

"When life knocks you down you have two choices-stay down or get up."

-Tom Krause

It was 6:00 in the morning. I was settled on the couch in the living room drowned profoundly in cerebration when suddenly a voice broke my eternal, not very productive and advancing, but still not completely meaningless chain of thoughts.

'Bhaiya would you like to have some tea'?

Saba was standing near the door with a cup in her hand.

Saba is my younger sister and was doing her B. Arch final year from a college in Lucknow. She had never been exceptional in her studies. But if you want to redesign your room, plan out a weekend in Shimla or looking for the opening line for your first meeting with one of the most beautiful girls in town, who is just completely out of your league, then Saba is the person to seek for.

'Ah haan, thanks Chotu', I said with a sudden craving for tea.

'Bhaiya,is everything alright'?

'Haan yaar, perfect'. It was not perfect at all, and my faint smile and miserable expressions blatantly exposed the attempted fabrication.

'Oye, is it again about your most awaited matrimony with that consummate celestial female?' Saba said with a mocking smile on her face.

'Shut up! Chotu,' and we started laughing.

Her guess was not completely out of mark. We have spent hours discussing the theoretically ideal girl and her most coveted qualities and I have always been hopeless at best according to Saba's conclusion. But this time the reason was very different.

'Chotu you know Aditya?'

'Yes, the tall and fair guy with curly hair. He is a friend of Samir.'

Samir is my younger brother. He was struggling to graduate as a Chemical Engineer from IIT Bombay.

'What about him?'

'He couldn't make it to IIT. He was a little upset.'

The second sentence was quite an understatement. Aditya was not just a little upset but totally wretched.

'But, you would have taken care of that Mr. Counselor.' The rationale of the appellation was perhaps my continuous volunteering for giving career advice and motivational speeches to people, especially students and that too especially engineers. According to

Saba, the people who can tolerate to listen to my sermons are the crème de la crème in courtesy and patience.

'No yaar it wasn't that easy. We spoke for around 45 minutes and I gave him all the logic and reasoning to explain the insignificance of the matter. And, for some time I even thought that he was convinced. But then, he said, '*whatever bhaiya, I won't be able to be an IITian in this incarnation.*'

'This line completely bowled me over. I could not even reply for a few seconds and that made the poor chap even sadder. He went away with a rather distressing but at the same time smug smile on his face.'

'He went away! And you let him go! Just like that!!' Saba sounded surprised

'Yaar, I did not know what to answer. I wanted time. I have called him today at 9:00 am to talk further on the issue. Whole night I was thinking about it. But I am still not sure how exactly I am going to deal with it.'

2

LAST NIGHT

The person who is waiting for something to turn up might start with his shirt sleeves.

–Garth Henrichs

"If at first you don't succeed, get a bigger hammer."

–Alan Lewis

Last Night:

I slept thinking about Aditya and trying to feel the level of his misery and dejection. At times I thought that he made sense and it was actually a very big loss. I was extremely disturbed and couldn't sleep properly. It was 03:30 am when I woke up and again the same thoughts started running in my mind. I was feeling pathetic. All these days have I been talking nonsense? Am I not even able to understand the problem? I kept on thinking for a while and when the burden became intolerable I decided to wake up my mother.

My mother has always been a great motivator and is always ready with convincing reasons for any depressed soul. She could have done well as a psychologist or a psychiatrist.

She was deep asleep. After persistent efforts she woke up and I told her the whole thing. She was tired and sleepy and had full right to be mad at me but at the same time she was conceited to have such a significant position in my life. It might be because of the latter that she showed magnanimity in accepting my apologies.

Then she started what she was best at, "Look Beta, the way I see it is that the guy is really depressed as he feels he has lost something forever; something, that was extremely desired and probably the most important thing for him at this point in life. But then there are a lot of people in a similar situation and rather I should say that almost everybody comes across similar kind of situation in life. Your father still regrets the fact that he could not play for the Indian cricket team.'

She went on like that for some more time and gave me quite a few more examples. I was listening to her spellbound. Satisfied with her explanation and seized by somnolence she said, 'Are you happy now? Was I able to answer you?'

'Yes,' came out the subconscious reply.

She kissed my forehead and went straight to bed. I was drowned into thoughts again. 'Was it really that simple?' 'Am I so dumb that I cannot even see such an obvious thing?' 'Is this argument strong enough to convince Aditya?' As soon as I thought of Aditya a lightning struck me and I could clearly see the obvious flaws in the argument.

I was feeling helpless. Next I thought of waking up my father. He generally wakes up at around 5:00 am and I thought of letting him complete his remaining 45 minutes of sleep. My impatience and agony soon overcame the feeling of sympathy and I went ahead to wake him up. He woke up easily and I narrated the situation in one breath.

He is a rather relaxed kind of a person. Sportsman by spirit he takes life, along with whole of its irregularity, on a very positive note. Positive living is healthy living and healthy living is happy living is his motto. He is an active member of many NGOs and other societies for Peace and Positive Attitude. If all his efforts are publicized properly then he might one day be nominated for some Peace Prize.

My father's response was very much as expected, 'Son, life is full of good things and bad things. Sometimes good things happen and sometimes bad things happen. We should keep our calm in both the situations. Great men conquer their emotions and stay unperturbed in happiness and sorrow. Try and empathize with the boy and tell him to stay calm and focus on his future.'

The answer was perfect. It could be a starting paragraph of a speech or the executive summary of a report. But here the audience was different. It wants a direct answer to an apparently simple question and is not interested in finding the hidden deep meaning of the golden words of my father.

We went out for a walk and he gave me other points in support of his stand. But to my misery all points were abstrusely philosophical and none was specific enough to face the question directly. We came back at around 5:30 am and I realized that I was essentially left with only three and a half hours.

I was doing nothing but thinking of some argument and then discarding it. Time went on and Aditya was to come at 9 am, I started feeling panicky. At that moment I realized that I still had access to two more people in the house and should try them out. Those two were my younger sister, Saba, and my younger brother, Samir.

Samir is a nocturnal animal and was still awake. He was enjoying his first summer break from IIT Bombay. I had suggested him to take up an internship under some professor at IIM Lucknow but he thought he was better off watching movies, surfing Orkut and chatting with his friends. I thought Samir might be of some help as he himself had recently gone through the pressure of IITJEE examination. Although he was lucky enough to clear but the stress and anxiety were tremendous.

My hopes rose a bit and with a little apprehension I went into his room. He was busy watching "Friends" and at the same time chatting with some other nocturnal animals. He appeared extremely occupied and didn't even notice me for some time. I was not in a state of mind to respect his privacy.

I made my presence felt and recounted the whole issue. Samir's response was very straightforward and to the poin,t.

He said, 'Bhai I agree with him that he wouldn't be able to be an IITian in this incarnation but then if there are positives and a lot of negatives also, of joining IIT. I am not much interested in Chemical Engineering but then I took it just because it was the best offered to me. After graduating I wish to work in some business consulting firm like you did and so these four years of rigorous grilling in Chemical Engineering would not fetch me anything.'

'We have very heavy curriculum here that requires a lot of effort to keep up with the class. Most of our time is wasted in reading and mugging things which we wouldn't even use for the second time in our life. On the contrary many other colleges in the country have relatively easier syllabus that gives students a lot of time to read as per their choice and to pursue their interests.'

He took a pause and said, 'You know bhai, it is because of this reason that I couldn't win that business plan contest in January. That team from Korenkar Institute of Technology was so versed with all the concepts; thanks to the amount of time they get after their regular classes. Here we have classes all day, and evenings are occupied with Labs.'

I gave him a nod and left the room.

3

NOT A GOOD START

There's nothing like biting off more than you can chew, and then chewing anyway.

–Mark Burnett

Don't be discouraged. It's often the last key in the bunch that opens the lock.

–Author unknown

As we were having tea I filled in Saba with everything. She listened very carefully and then started thinking. One can often see her very deep in her thoughts and the outcomes can range from changing the color of her nails to repainting the walls, or from a romantic poem (with imbalanced verses) on the enigmatic nature of life to absolute nothing. She finally broke the silence

'Bhaiya, you guys are overconfident, overpriced morons'

'Excuse me, what happened? Which guys?' I was appalled.

'Well, you IITians I mean. You all are self-obsessed, attention-seeking B…' Saba was at her full rage.

'Hey, listen Chotu just chill yaar. I should not have asked you this question. I know it was a little too much for you.' Immediately after speaking I realized I have crossed the line there. But the realization was already late and 'BANG' a speeding fist landed on my stomach.

'Ouch, Chotu sorry yaar, but why did you insult my fraternity?' I tried to defend my outrageous statement but the situation was way beyond control.

'Because you deserve it. Happy now!! Now get out of my way.' She went away as I made a few futile attempts to stop her.

I felt bad for upsetting her in the morning. But then I consoled myself by thinking about how stupid she was to call every IITian as overconfident, overpriced and attention-seeking. Girls are meant to be dumb and I was just a little unfair in putting that in loud words.

4

ADITYA

The most glorious moments in your life are not the so-called days of success, but rather those days when out of dejection and despair you feel rise in you a challenge to life, and the promise of future accomplishments.

– Gustav Flaubert

Work is worship.

–Author unknown

'Bhaiya', 'bhaiya'..came a voice from somewhere. I was not sure whether it was real or I was in my dreams. I saw Saba standing next to me and with her was Aditya.

'Sorry bhaiya, I think I disturbed you. You called me at 9:00. I told didi that it was just fine and I could wait for some time.' It was 8:45 am and Aditya had already come. I could not clearly remember when I fell asleep. I woke up and straight away went to the living room.

Now it was just me and Aditya sitting in the living room. I was lying on the couch and he was placed straight back on the sofa.

'Well young man, yesterday we could not complete the discussion. So, what were you saying?' I pretended as if I am not even aware of the nuclear missile that hit my country yesterday.

'Bhaiya, I am just too sad and depressed. I think all my efforts and every sacrifice went in vain.'

'Hmmmm.'

'I think I am really not worth anything and I am just a jerk. If I cannot get something for which I worked so hard then I cannot get anything ever in my life. I have to accept it now that I can never be successful. I am a useless person and I hate myself. There is no point living like such a loser. Everything is finished. Everything is over....over..' Before even finishing the sentence he started whimpering.

'Hey hey, Aditya, what happened? Trust me its not that big.' For some time I tried all that *'it's going to be alright' 'you don't have to worry about it'* and other similar crap but all in vain. There was pain and there was quite a lot of it. Although I could probably not gauge the actual intensity but I could certainly vouch that it was not very easy to manage for a sensitive teenager.

He kept on wailing for a few minutes and all my attempts to console failed miserably. At last I said, 'Hey that's it, you know what, I think you are right. You have really lost your chance. You could not make it and now there is nothing left.'

I don't know why I said that. But to my surprise it clicked. At least he calmed down. Now it was my turn to calm down and composing myself I said, 'I am sorry. I understand. It is and it really is very big and important.' I told him in a very relaxed and soothing tone.

'I remember what my symptoms before IITJEE exams were.' I never thought that I would ever be telling this to anyone for the obvious reason of getting embarrassed. But somehow it just came out.

'One month for the exam and I used to cry every alternate day; sometimes for not being able to solve a question, sometimes for not being able to wake up early; sometimes for not sleeping properly; sometimes for not sticking to my routine; sometimes for scoring low marks in mock tests and sometimes just for the sake of crying.'

I took a deep breath. I knew there were million more reasons for which I used to get upset and some of them could not be even mentioned.

I continued, 'You know when only a week was left for the exam, I was so terrified that I fainted in my room. My parents had to break open the door and rush me to a hospital.'

While I was telling him all this I went so deep into my memories that for a second I experienced the same sensation and goosebumps appeared on my skin. Recollecting myself I said, 'So dear, you see you are not the only one who gets nervous. We all feel the same way and it was just a matter of chance that I was a bit lucky on the day that counts.'

'Now the question is that just because of that one unlucky day have you actually lost everything? Everything which you have done is actually in vain? And whatever else negative you think is that all true just because of that one bad day?'

He was looking at me with his empty eyes.

'You know let us say, yes you had a really big loss or say you lost everything. You cannot get the best thing because you were unlucky or you did not study much or you are dumb or just that you were not meant for it or whatever other stupid reason.'

There was a very strong possibility that he might think that I am a complete jerk but I still continued.

'You can never be an IITian in this incarnation and can never achieve anything great. I accept everything as you put it. Really big loss! I will have to agree.'

It was really easy to guess that if I continue a little longer he was going to break down. But then I was working according to a good plan or at least what I thought was a good plan.

Seeing the first tear in his eyes I got a bit nervous and said, 'Everything's accepted now what's next?'

I sipped my tea again and picked up a sandwich (courtesy Saba). The sandwich was really tasty or may be it tasted amazing as it was after a long time that I realized that Homo sapiens need to eat to continue their metabolism. So as a generous gesture I said loudly, 'Nice sandwich Chotu.'

'It was for Aditya', came Saba's retort like a guided ammunition straight from the kitchen.

Only the bravest men, maniacs or Samir have the guts for a comeback for this one. It is never easy to make Saba let go things. I often keep on apologizing for my mistakes of yore (when she reminds me of the same). I still have to make up for spoiling the cover of her notebook when she was in ninth grade.

'Bhaiya, honestly speaking I don't know what is next. I am really not in a state of mind right now to think of anything.'

His voice was for a change had a touch of reason and sensibility in it. I felt happy.

'But whatever I do, it will not be even close to what I could have done in IIT,' he said in a depressing note.

'Hmmmm, Aditya yaar I think now I am able to see your problem more clearly. I can try and give you a lot of logic and explanations but they might not sound very convincing to you right now.'

I was really thinking hard to match his arguments. I could realize there was something missing but just could not figure it out. I was getting a little frustrated. It was kind of hitting on my ego. I consider myself a good and convincing speaker, I had been into consulting for so many years, influencing people with my arguments is my job and here I am, feeling helpless in front of an eighteen year old.

5

YASH

If you feel you are down on your luck, check the level of your effort.

–Robert Brault

Effort is a commitment to seeing a task through to the end, not just until you get tired of it .

–Howard Cate

'Bhai, can I come in.' Samir was standing at the door. He came like an angel for me. I so wanted a break.

'Didn't you sleep at all' I asked as generally Samir is in his deepest state of sleep at this hour.

'No, just for two hours', he replied casually.

Somehow when you are in college less sleep is considered something worth flaunting. Samir and Aditya were friends from coaching. They started talking and I sneaked out for some time.

I went to Saba's room and told her that I am sorry for what I said in the morning. To my surprise she said it was alright. As I was coming out of her room she said, 'bhaiya Aditya is really very sad.' Too much sympathy for every living (and non-living) being is her another problem.

'Ya Chotu, he is.' I said and took a sip from the bottle of Pepsi in her room.

'So, are you able to make him understand that it is not that big a thing in the long run?'

I did not reply and just nodded in an un-interpretable manner.

'Bhaiya, you yourself think like that, isn't it.'

'Like what Chotu.' Then it hit.

'No! oh no! no!' I said in a strange tone.

'You do bhaiya, you do and it is so obvious and it is soooooo stupid.' The second so was so stretched that if you add the number of 'letter Os' required to spell it then it can probably be the longest word.

But I don't know was it the length of so or her expressions or something else which made me think that do I actually believe that it is not that big a loss.

Saba continued, 'What if not IIT. There are a million more ways to be where one wants to; there are a million more things that bring anyone at par with IITians in the field of ones' choice; and there are a billion more things that help one surpass IITians in the field they are working in. It is actually not the institute but the person. You keep telling me this big-shot is from IIT Kanpur that big-shot is from IIT Bombay and someone else from some other IIT. But bhaiya they are not even one percent of the big-shots I know with my very limited quantum of knowledge. Not only this, most of the big names I know are big for me just because you have told me so. So if you remove them from my list then the percentage of successful IITians in the total number of successful people I know would not even have a natural number if I go for two or even three significant digits. So dear brother wake up and come out of your obsession.'

It took me sometime to regain my normal senses. Things like who am I, whom am I talking to, what are we talking about and what the heck she just said started coming into my mind as if I was recovering from a memory loss. This probably happened because Saba was talking in the language of a subject she detested ever since or may be because my mind had just opened to new doors of information and knowledge.

She continued, 'Or you know what, call up your boss. Probably he might help you out. Oh I remember he is younger than you and he is not an IITian. Ouchh!! Oh man! How did this happen? Don't your seniors know that IITians are the best and they deserve just the best treatment and anyone from any other college can never be ahead of any IITian.' If sarcasm was a liquid then the amount which was flowing was enough to flood the city.

But, she had a point, quite a valid point. It instigated a whole new thought process in my mind, as if the things were clearing out. I kissed Saba on her forehead and left the room. I did not even wait to enjoy her surprised expressions which are generally quite amusing.

I wanted to go to the living room full of enthusiasm and energy like a soldier rushing to the battlefield, but had to go somewhere else. I spent a good 20 minutes in the washroom. It helped me in arranging my thoughts and arguments.

After coming out, I went to the living room where Aditya was sitting alone. He was sad and depressed on his "huge loss". The worse part was that he believed that he could not make for his loss ever, when in reality there was no loss at all, and the worse part was that his belief, his sadness and his despair now had the potential to inflict some real irreparable loss.

'Hey' I tried sounding cheerful and friendly.

'So where were....'

'Bhaiya, Yash bhaiya on phone', came Saba's voice.

'Ok Chotu coming.'

I went inside to answer the call.

Yash is my closest friend, more like my alter ego. We have quite a bit in common; we like similar places, we enjoy similar things, we both love SRK (though I mimic better), we are very good at acting and therefore both are good liars and so on. Although here is an irony worth mentioning I did not like Yash's girl friend for years.

Call took me around 15 minutes. I came back to the living room. Aditya was sitting deep in his thoughts.

'Sorry yaar, you know Yash, he can really take a lot of time.' I said casually.

'What young man thinking about your girl friend.' I tried sounding candid but he rightly gave me a "you are sounding stupid" look. And as expected he asked, 'what were you saying bhaiya?'

'Well.... Yes...actually you might find this a little crazy but I don't believe that it is a loss and in fact I believe that it is a blessing. It is a blessing in disguise. Yes Aditya I believe that it is a blessing but not many people are able to understand and appreciate it.'

The look on Aditya's face was a near perfect depiction of the word 'confusion'.

I continued, 'sometimes we think that certain thing is bad just because everybody around us thinks that it is bad. We do not even care to think that whether it is actually bad for us and if at all it is then how bad it is or how much harm can it do to us.'

'Bhaiya I am sorry but what are you talking about? You cannot say that not getting into IIT is not bad for me or it is a blessing.'

I could see that Aditya was getting mad at me. I continued, 'I heard you, but I would still say that yes it was good for you. It is a blessing for you just that you are not able to appreciate this thing.'

'Bhaiya I respect you and I know you have had much more experience than I have but I am sorry I am not in a state of mind to listen to your philosophical ideologies. I know what all are coming next, that it is just a test and life has to offer much bigger challenges, our failures make us strong and we learn a lot of things from them. So failing early in life is actually good for us it helps us in analyzing ourselves at an early stage and we end up becoming a better and more successful human being – and all other similar crap.'

Gosh! He said that in a single breath and as far as I can guess these probably were the words of his father.

'Pretty well,' said Aditya' I agree with you. If I would had been in your place even I would not have listened to that crap. So I am not going to tell you any such thing. I am going to prove it to you that not getting into IIT actually is not that bad and in fact might be turned into a blessing. And trust me this would be a purely objective and practical proof based on actual facts and figures and absolutely no philosophical angle attached.'

'As far as I am concerned I am convinced with what I am saying but I understand that it is very difficult for you to appreciate. I was discussing the matter with Yash and we came out with the idea that let us talk one by one about all the things that you think you could have got and have now missed by not being able to get through IITJEE.'

'Yash must be here any moment. In the meantime let us list down the things that you think you have missed by not getting through IITJEE. Yes, now tell me one by one about your unfathomable losses.'

Aditya was not expecting that the questions could be directed towards him also. He was a little surprised by this. After some time he said, 'bhaiya I don't know why are you doing this? I think you know very well what all have I lost but still if you want me to tell you then fine I will definitely list down my unfathomable losses.'

Anger was dripping from his voice.

'I think you must be having a very fair idea of how much respect IITian get from the society. They get special treatment, their views are valued and people have more trust in them and it is just because you are an IITian that I am here to seek your help.' Aditya said this and the same smug smile again came on his face.

The statement was utter crap and so was it treated.

'This is absolute rubbish. You don't get respect just because you are an IITian you get respect on the basis of your achievements. Getting selected in IIT is considered to be an achievement in the society. Some think that it is a big deal as it is very difficult to get through, some think that it is just completely out of the world and the best possible thing to do and some even go to the extent that they think that if one doesn't have IIT then one can never do anything in life.'

My last line was obviously pointing towards him.

'But that is all thinking', I continued, 'it doesn't change anything. It is an extremely short term achievement and an even shorter recognition. What actually matters is where you end up being in your life.'

As I ended I realized that Aditya was not convinced. As I was trying to hide my frustration I heard,

'It is still an achievement so there actually is a loss. So there are some people who actually think that it might not be the biggest loss but still it is a loss, a short term small loss. But I would really love to have a short term small loss if that gives me a long term big gain.'

It was not Aditya but Yash. He was standing at the door with a can of soft drink, his usual trademark, in his hand.

He walked towards us and continued, 'If you take my perspective on this then actually being an IITian is definitely a small short term social achievement, but at the same time in the long run it is not that desired.'

'After IIT if you are successful then you are successful because you are an IITian, so no big deal and no big social achievement but in case you are not as successful as your peers then you end up in frustration and the same society mocks you. If you are not an IITian and you are successful then you get to have all the credit and no useless pressures. At the end of the day what you have achieved in life is important. And with the similar level of achievement one gets more social respect if one is not from IIT.'

He took a pause and said, 'But my dear friend, this stupid argument is for only those stupid people whom you referred to in your argument, people for whom IIT decides your social achievement.'

Yash continued, 'So Adityaji, I hope I answered your question. Having said that I would say that it is actually not important what people think or how much importance they attach to small achievements. And sir how many of the successful people, who are praised by the society, are from IIT. I have studied there for four years and still not even 1% of the total number of people I admire are from IIT.'

'Where the hell are you coming from Mr. Uninvited?'

'Oh I come straight from the lands of politeness and hospitality Mr. Rudy.'

The atmosphere got lighter and Saba and my mother also came in the living room.

Mamma asked if we would like to eat anything and when she got no direct answer she asked Saba to get some more sandwiches and cold drinks.

'So, Aditya I think that was quite an answer to your question. But I understand you must be having a lot more of them still left.'

I could figure out that he was happy to hear our words but not even close to getting convinced. His pain and agony was visible in his eyes. The helplessness was scary.

'Fine bhaiya, I agree social things might not be the most important but if we move on to the practical aspects then IITians have a better career and a better professional life.'

'Well and who says that?' I replied.

'Statistics' snapped Yash.

'Yeah and there is absolutely no doubt about that. You can pick up any batch of IIT and compare it with its contemporary batches of other colleges and it would win hands down in terms of career, status and professional achievements of the students', added Aditya.

'Yes definitely' said Yash.

Although both of them were ganging up on me but I liked the vigour and enthusiasm in Aditya's voice.

I said, 'I should say that it is quite an impressive argument, but my friends the prosperity of any batch of IIT has nothing to do with them being IITians. It is a bunch of intelligent and motivated people who would anyways reach those high altitudes. I think you should ask more specific questions.'

'Or may be before he asks any more questions you should analyze this question further-bhaiya.' Saba was back with cold drinks and snacks.

She continued 'Are these people actually more successful? Are all the IITians exceptionally successful or is it just a few of them. What have these people done to be that successful? I think these are some obvious questions. Aren't they bhaiya?'

Saba is no doubt sarcasm personified but this discussion was helping me in giving words to my thoughts and may be to Yash's also, as he said, 'I think Saba is right, we should pick up some exceptionally successful IITians and then try and analyze their recipe of success. It might help us in estimating the contribution of IIT in their success.'

'Or may be Yash bhaiya we should first broadly classify the areas in which students generally move after IIT and analyze them so that we get a clearer picture of the impeccable impact of IIT in shaping the destinies of these superbly successful mortals.'

The venomous sarcasm was purely deliberate but we could do nothing but acknowledge the better strategy.

'Ahem…yessss…Ahem…that's even better', stammered Yash.

'As far as I think there are four major routes that students take. A good percentage goes for MS (Masters in Science) abroad, some of them go for their MBA, a rare few go for entrepreneurship and the rest settle for jobs.'

'As I was thinking of any other possible career option,' Yash added, 'Dude you left out a few categories, which incidentally form quite a large percentage; those who flunk and get their degrees extended, those who flunk very often and get terminated and those who are able to graduate but are not placed in any company for job or selected in any university for higher studies.'

'Ohh yes, you are right and now there actually is one more category which comprises students who take a break for civil services preparation,' I added casually and picked up a sandwich.

'IITians do not get job or get selected in any university. How is that possible? And why do they take break for civil services preparation? I used to think they get selected in their first attempt.' Aditya spoke with anxiety.

'Well allow me to introduce you to the reality. In my batch around 30 students were studying for civil services full time and only four got finally selected and that too not with a great rank.' Yash spoke it casually but Aditya was very serious and asked curiously, 'What are the rest of them doing?'

'Well as far as I know two more have got selected and the rest have either gone for higher studies, settled with some job or are still trying.'

Aditya was giving very confused expressions. It was probably difficult for him to believe that IITians, whom he regards just next to God, can land up in this mess also.

Saba who was quiet for some time said, 'bhaiya these might be some exceptional cases, lets discuss the broad areas that you mentioned.'

'Right, let us start with your area of interest Aditya. What do you want to do after your engineering?'

'I always wanted to do my engineering from IIT Kanpur, then my MBA from IIM Ahmedabad and then land up in my dream job.'

That was an incredibly direct and straightforward answer. Even after working for so many years I didn't have this level of clarity for my career and Yash's face confirmed his presence in the same camp.

Yash was the first one to respond, 'Very well said, so your final objective is your dream job for which IIM Ahmedabad and IIT Kanpur are your stepping stones.'

Aditya gave a slight nod and Yash continued, 'let us analyze these stepping stones step by step. We can write your perfect equation of success as:

IIT Kanpur + IIM Ahmedabad = Dream Job

We engineers love to see things in the form of equation and that's probably the reason of our terrible failure when it comes to relationships.

'Let us analyze the first step – contribution of IIT Kanpur. Now, as you are getting the job after IIM Ahmedabad then IIT can affect it in two possible ways: helping you in getting the job or helping you in getting through IIM.'

Yash was explaining with an amazing blend of passion and vigour and Aditya's attention level was giving a tough competition to that of the students sitting in the front row of Professor Isaac Newton's lecture on the laws of gravity.

'Placement takes place in the second year so clearly employers would be more interested in student's present profile and their achievements in IIM than their royal blood line of the geeks of IIT. Second point…'

'May I' I interrupted Yash in between, 'may I explain the second point.'

'Ohh yes, sure go ahead.'

'Second point is that, does it really help you in getting through IIM. So, my dear friend it can be easily proved that it does not.' I took a little pause and then started again.

'In IIT the curriculum is little on the higher side and the campus is full of geeks. First you don't get enough time to focus on your CAT preparation and secondly and more importantly is that IIMs give weight to your CGPA, which obviously suffer in IIT as the grading is relative and the geek community wants' A' grade even more than they want have a date with Monica Bellucci or....'

I controlled my emotional overflow and Yash was smiling as he knew how much I hated when my grades used to get screwed because of the perpetual study machines – who used to do the courses with us.

'Hey and just to add on to this even after a 99.81 percentile in CAT I didn't get a call from IIM Bangalore for interview as I was a five point someone', blurted Yash with his voice full of detest.

'They are not bothered which college you belong to but only the grades you have. They are...'

Aditya interrupted Yash and spoke excitingly, 'I am sorry but do you mean to say that if I am having 80% in any other college then I am better off than a 60% in IIT.'

'Anyday,' we both said together.

'It is true Aditya and somewhere we also think that it is unfair but so is life', came out Yash's dejected voice.

Yash has been trying for his MBA from quite some time but he could not make it to the college of his choice. He scored 99.81 percentile in CAT 2005 and 99.75 percentile in CAT 2006 but still could not get through A B or C (IIM Ahmedabad, IIM Bangalore or IIM Calcutta) and he blames his grades and IIT Delhi for it.

'Honestly bhaiya it is still not making much sense to me. How can IIT be a hindrance in getting through IIM? Number of IITians in any of the IIMs is overwhelmingly greater than that from any other college. Therefore in some way it must actually be providing help in getting through IIMs.'

His words were full of confidence. He was probably thinking that why the hell these stupid people cannot comprehend simple statistics.

While I was giving words to my thought Yash burst out, 'O! Omniscient, is it because of the secret elixir, for cracking IIMs, of the hidden well on the sacred grounds of the heavenly place called IIT or are you talking about the legend of the prophecy of the witches of lake Enara.'

After a noticeable delay Aditya gave a flabbergasted expression accompanied by a barely audible sound which was probably of the 'come again' or 'beg your pardon domain'.

'Aditya, he means that IIT is not giving you any special help. It just has a high percentage of focussed and hardworking students.'

Before I could say anything else Yash said, 'They don't get into IIM because they are from IIT but because of the countless hours of slogging, because of months of sleepless nights and because of the motivation and consistency. And I can bet the seven wonders of this planet that any student from any college if puts in the equivalent effort, given no major difference in mental abilities, would definitely achieve similar results.'

There was a lot of passion and conviction in his words. As Aditya was trying to comprehend I said, 'Aditya I will tell you a very interesting story in this context. In 2005 six students of a Hindi medium college of my village Amroha – a place near Moradabad – cleared CAT and made it to different IIMs. One of them happens to be my cousin. He has done his MBA from IIM Ahmedabad. He was just like any other ordinary guy of his college until him and his friends decided to take their lives on a different road. With their hard work and perseverance they were able to realize their first goal towards success.'

'But, bhaiya these exceptions always exist. Some of these people are gifted and some are sheer lucky.'

That was a brutal assault of my brilliant and well thought argument. I was really out of any other statement in support of my point but I could not let the hard earned and well deserved achievement of my dear cousin to be branded as a mere benevolence of lady luck.

'If you want I can get him to talk to you. Would you like to talk to him?'

Aditya was not expecting this. He gave a thoughtful expression and with a pinch of excitement said, 'Now!!!'

'Ya, why not? Right here, right now.'

'OK.' He tried to sound as cool and composed as he could.

6

ANVAR

Opportunity is missed by most people because it is dressed in overalls and looks like work.

–Thomas Edison

Men are made stronger on realization that the helping hand they need is at the end of their own arm.

–Sidney J. Phillips

I asked Yash to call up my cousin Anwar and fill him with the situation. Anwar is presently working with one of the best consulting firms with an annual salary quite higher compared to mine. There were times when he was not able to pay for his correspondence course for CAT preparation. I was briefing Aditya about Anwar when Yash came back with the cordless handset in his hand.

'I have briefed him of the situation. I am putting him on loudspeaker.'

'Hey Anwar, how are you?' It was after quite a long time that I was talking to him.

'I am fine. What's up with you?'

'My life is without spice as usual. Anyway, here is a friend of mine who wants to talk to you. Would you please tell him how you made it to IIM Ahmedabad?'

'Yeah, definitely. Hello Aditya.'

'Hello Anwar bhaiya'

'So tell me mate what help my useless soul can offer you?'

One of the several qualities I admire in Anwar is his modesty. He might have turned into a big gun from a no one but that has not corrupted his demeanour.

'How did you make it to IIM Ahmedabad?'

'Hmmm....Ok. That was quite straightforward. Yaar, those are the most memorable days of my life. Sahil must have mentioned how pathetic I was in studies. I was careless towards life and never used to give a serious thought to my future. But my biggest problem was my utmost satisfaction with the situation.' Anwar's tone was suggesting that he was getting nostalgic.

'It was the January of the second year of graduation when we six – five of my friends and me – sat together to discuss our future. It was in that discussion that we realized how directionless we were and how uncertain our future was. With the huge amount of responsibility on our shoulders it became even more imperative to do something meaningful in life. The road ahead was dark and scary. After a long discussion and then subsequent sittings and guidance from our seniors and teachers we concluded that CAT is one good start off point.'

His voice went on getting deeper and Aditya's concentration went on increasing and his ear kept closing in towards the handset.

'Then started the preparation phase – for eight months we studied for 6 hours daily from 10 pm to 4 am. We shared our resources, our knowledge and helped each other to improve. It was an uphill task as we were from Hindi medium and CAT focusses a lot on English. But we did not give up and kept on putting our best efforts. In the end our efforts paid off and we all secured above 99.5 percentile. Similarly, we put our best foot forward for the interview preparation and all of us were able to manage a seat in Indian Institute of Management.'

I have heard this story quite a few times but it still gives me goosebumps and defies a lot of stupid social notions.

'And where are the rest of the guys?' Yash asked Anwar.

'Well, Rajat and Salim are in US and Anirudh is in Hongkong, in different financial advisory organizations and the rest are in India.'

'Just to add Rajat got President's gold medal in IIMA.' I said softly.

'Yeah...and he also got one of the most sought after jobs,' added Anwar. 'It is actually very difficult to believe when you remember the time when he was struggling to secure the minimum percentage marks in graduation required to get admission in an IIM.'

'I think if six below average students from a Hindi medium school of a small town can get through IIMs then anyone with focussed efforts can.'

Smile on Aditya's face was priceless. We continued talking to Anwar and listening to his experiences for some more time and then thanked him for his time and advice.

Yash said, 'I remember when I was in first year there was a senior who got calls from all the IIMs but could not join as he got an F grade in his B.Tech project and his degree got extended.'

'There are a lot more cases like this', I backed Yash. 'Once in IIT Kharagpur a professor kept the mid sem exam on the day of CAT exam. IIT professors do not appreciate MBA very much and I don't think they are wrong in doing so given the amount of money government is spending on engineers.'

'But that's unfair professors cannot put midsem on the day of CAT exam.' Aditya showed his skepticism with confidence.

'Dude! Trust me! they can.' Yash's tone was full of hatred – may be for the system or for his project guide whom he held responsible for screwing up his first attempt at CAT.

There was silence for some time. Yash probably was again repeating his exercise of analyzing the factors that went wrong in his first attempt. Aditya seemingly was compassing the quantum of new informational inflow. I was trying to guess Aditya's next question and preparing my answer for it.

After some time Aditya finally spoke, 'bhaiya that means if I prepare properly I can get through CAT and get selected in IIM Ahmedabad regardless of the college I join.'

'Yes exactly', said Yash and looked at me. We were happy but the happiness was short-lived. It was a very small battle of the big war we were about to face.

7

'A' STANDS FOR ANJALI

Much good work is lost for the lack of a little more.

–Edward H. Harriman

God gives every bird its food, but He does not throw it into its nest.

–J.G. Holland.

'But bhaiya that's for MBA. A lot of other students as you said want to go for further studies in their field of interest. I have heard it becomes easier to get admittance and scholarship if one has recommendation from an IIT Professor.'

'Although I do not agree with you completely but I have to say you have quite a good knowledge about things', I said casually.

'Actually Anjali told me that. She was in my coaching with me and is very upset as she also couldn't make it to IIT.'

'Anjaliiii....Anjali Mathur....is she – blue eyes, blunt cut shoulder touching hair, fancy caps, amazing....'

'Dude', I shouted, 'relax, there are a million Anjali's out there.'

'I think Yash bhaiya is right.' I also knew that he was right but I did not want to make it obvious. She was a diva. We saw her once in the coaching and later found out through our sources that she lives in our sector only. Yash finds her strikingly similar to Anjali Sharma of the first half of 'Kuch Kuch Hota Hai.'

'What does she want to do?' Yash was the commandant now.

'She is more inclined towards research and wants to do her PhD in Artificial Intelligence from Stanford University. She is very upset as she thinks that all her dreams are shattered and now she would never be able to get what she wants. She thinks her life is ruined.'

'Bullllllll Shit...,' Yash shouted with annoyance, 'an amazingly beautiful teenage girl has dreamt of everything she wants from her life and all of that is already shattered. Nonsense!'

'Bhaiya, she is really upset and is not even eating and talking properly after the result.'

'What the hell,' I also got a little vexed, 'who the heck told her that no Indian can do a PhD in AI from Stanford if he is not from IIT. You know what – on my second day in the campus one of my senior said, *"Sahil, you have cleared IIT; parents, friends and everybody else in the society must be very happy for you; your ego balloon must have bloated to new dimensions; trust me this is all IIT has got to offer. For anything extra from here you have to start all over again."* I couldn't appreciate his words at that time but now I fully understand the truth in them. I was unfortunate to learn it the hard way.'

'Hey Aditya she lives nearby why don't you call her here', Yash said casually.

Boys will be boys. But not all wishes come true.

'She would be happy to come.'

But some do.

'Sahil bhaiya, I told her that I was going to meet you. She also wanted to come but was skeptical as she has never talked to you and you might not even know her.'

Soothing winds of joy and blush started drifting inside me. Controlling my emotions was the toughest task at hand.

'Yes, he might not know her but I don't think that makes much of a difference. She is our junior and we would be happy if we can be of any help to her.' Yash's timing was perfect and I got enough moments to compose myself again.

'Ok bhaiya, then I will call her.'

Before Aditya could go to call Anjali, Saba called us all for lunch. We all had lunch. Aditya was a lot more cheerful.

After lunch, Aditya went to call Anjali; Yash and I came back to the living room.

'Do you have a light blue T-shirt?' Yash asked.

'Why'

'Girls generally like blue'

'Shut up, yaar.'

'Just kidding. What are you going to tell her?'

'The reality.'

'As in?'

'Don't you remember Shikha and Suvir,' I said excitingly.

'The students from Northern College of Engineering Sciences who won the Annual Technical Paper Presentation Contest,' replied Yash.

'And got a hundred percent scholarship for MS from Massachusetts Institute of technology', I added.

MIT was a shattered dream for me. I always wanted to get a Ph.D. in alternate energy from there but my poor grades and bad reputation among the professors made it impossible for me.

'But seriously Sahil, here again statistics might not be very favorable. On top of it, now there will be two of them for us to convince and the new person belongs to the category with which we are not very good when it comes to convincing.'

'Hey…how can you say that?' I replied in disagreement.

'Statistics!!!' replied Yash and we both started laughing.

We definitely don't fall into the 'charmers' category' but our experiences have been even worse than what we deserve. Sonal (Yash's girlfriend) was a serendipity and I was still waiting for the cupid's blessings.

We started discussing our past experiences in the field and Yash began retelling his much repeated stories and wildest adventures. This went on for a good fifteen minutes when the door bell rang; Aditya, and moments later Anjali, entered the living room with Saba.

Anjali was a little different from the image we had. She wasn't in her typical jeans, t-shirt and cap combination but instead she was wearing a blue choodidaar salwar suit. I realized that 'her dressing style makes her special' was actually our misconception and it was the other way round.

'Hi, Sahil bhaiya', she said in her sweet voice before sitting on the sofa in front of me on the other side of the center table.

I gathered all the scattered pieces of my consciousness and replied back.

She said, 'bhaiya I am sorry I came just like that without…….'

Before she could finish I said, 'That's perfectly alright. I am happy that you thought I could be helpful' and tried to give her the best possible expression, which I guess, on the basis of the movements of my facial muscles and the look on Yash's face, was probably not even close to what was intended.

'So Anjali what's up with you? How have you been?' Yash casually asked Anjali.

'Hmmm.....not great I would say.'

'And why would someone your age say that?'

'Bhaiya....I....I...,' a drop of crystal clear liquid sat on her eyelid for a moment before landing on the table.

Anjali didn't say anything for some time neither did anyone else did. She finally spoke, 'You very well know what happened. Don't you? I can never be an IITian in this incarnation.'

I stared at Aditya, as a culprit for spreading the virus, but he pointed towards her with a gesture of *'she only told me that'*.

'Oh Dear Goddess, was being in IIT the only purpose of your incarnation.'

Sarcasm doesn't work best with girls and that too especially with beautiful girls and even more when they are depressed as well. She started crying.

'Hey...hey...hey...what happened?' Yash croaked bewildered. Intentional ignorance often puts one into such situations. And if you are into it with a beautiful girl then there are rules – you cannot raise your voice above her; cannot speak any meaningful statement due to the unknown fear of worse; cannot leave the scene and YOU CANNOT TOUCH. Thankfully he was abiding by all the rules and croaking comprised mostly of *Hey*, *Sorry* and *Please*. My best friend was facing one of his worst nightmares.

We were clueless and I decided to sit quietly to avoid any further damage. Aditya tried to console Anjali while Yash was helplessly apologizing for his heinous crime. Aditya gave her a glass of water.

She drank it and then covered her face in her handkerchief. After few moments she removed the handkerchief, apologized and sat gloomily. Now I knew that for her the explanation has to be really smooth and easily comprehensible.

So I started in a very explanatory tone, 'Not clearing an examination doesn't put a question mark on our abilities neither does it reduces our potential in any manner but I would agree that it comes as a major setback for most of us. I don't think that it should have such a huge impact on your life. You were just a little bit unlucky for those few critical hours.'

I explained Anjali everything patiently as I have told Aditya. She did not speak in between but was very attentive. After carefully listening to me for quite some time she finally said, 'bhaiya I always wanted to do my Artificial Intelligence PhD from Stanford and work further in the field. I would never be able to do it now.'

'Why would you think like that?' I said very calmly. I was putting in a conscious effort to keep my voice cool and composed to abide by the law of 'dealing with beautiful girls.'

'Bhaiya, Stanford takes the best among the best students from India. Only a very few IITians are able to make let aside the non IITians.'

'Who gave you these Statistics?' I said this very softly so that it doesn't sound offensive.

'My cousin has graduated from IIT Bombay. He wanted to do his PhD from Stanford but even after having good grades and good recommendations from the professors he could not make it. If such good students from IIT are not able to make it then for others it is just a dream I suppose.' Her sadness made it quite clear that she strongly believed each and every word she just said.

'Have you gone through the admission process of Stanford University?

'No.'

'What are they looking for and what kind of students do they take?'

'No, but isn't it obvious that they would want to take students from the best colleges of the country.'

'Fine, is this the only criteria or is it their most important criteria.'

'May be.'

'May be.....if you say that you have lost something forever then I expect a more informed answer from you.'

She was quiet. I waited for some time and then spoke.

'Anjali......the goals of life are not even a bit dependent upon such small things. Do you think every Indian who makes it to Stanford is form IIT or for that matter everybody who make it to Stanford from other countries are from the best universities. To extend it further a bit all the people who have done great work in Artificial Intelligence are all of them from Stanford.'

'But bhaiya don't you agree it would have been easier if I was in IIT.'

'May be or may be not', I replied coldly.

'I know a lot of people who are not from IIT and have made it to the best universities.'

'There is a very close friend of mine Saraswat Ahuja who did his engineering from some college in Bengal and then went to Princeton for his PhD in engine design. There is another close friend who went to Carnegie-Mellon University and he also wasn't from IIT.'

'Bhaiya there are a very few lucky cases like this.'

'Who told you this? Have you ever seen the statistics of top foreign universities? I don't deny that there are quite a few IITians but then there are significant number of students from others colleges too.'

We were giving logics, citing examples and using the best available ammunition but the enemy's castle – the castle of misconception – was just too strong. The discussion was proceeding on an endless road. So I decided to bring in some objectivity.

'Ok Anjali let me put a simple comparison in front of you. Let there be two applicant to Stanford Artificial Intelligence PhD; A and B. A is from IIT with a CGPA of 9.0 and got inclined towards AI somewhere in his junior year, whereas B is from some other college. He is a topper there and had been throughout working in the field of Artificial Intelligence; and with regular efforts has also been able to publish a paper on AI. Not only this B has been in touch with top AI people of top Universities of the world though emails and taking their guidance on various issues.'

I took a pause and then said, 'How much out of 10 do you think Stanford Admission Committee would give to A and B.'

She was not prepared for this and therefore gave me a confused but at the same time intriguing look, and uttered softly, 'no idea.' There was a little flash of smile on her face and that was more than enough to boost up my confidence.

I smiled back and said, 'Even in the worst case B gets at least one point more than A.'

8

'A' ALSO STANDS FOR AUDREY

Work spares us from three evils: boredom, vice, and need.

– Voltaire

Unless you are willing to drench yourself in your work beyond the capacity of the average man, you are just not cut out for positions at the top.

– JC Penny

Saba entered the room. She is quite a fan of Anjali. Samir has been keeping her updated about her stylish caps, fancy haircuts, iconic accessories and mind blowing dresses.

'Hi, Saba Di.'

Attention is adorable especially when it comes from someone even more adorable.

'Hello Anjali. How have you been?'

They got into the normal, usual, boring, senseless but omnipresent girl talk. They had exchanged only a few girlie courtesy statements before I interrupted.

'Saba, are you in touch with Audrey, Audrey Conceicao. I was wondering if we could make her talk to Anjali.'

'Oh yes bhaiya, I am, in fact she gave me a call yesterday. I will just check with her', and she rushed out of the room.

Blessed are those whom Saba helps with such eagerness.

'Which college is Audrey from?' uttered Yash.

'Presently she is pursuing her Masters in Science in Chemical Engineering from Princeton University', I replied.

'And where did she do her graduation from?' asked Yash.

'Not from IIT, or NIT, or REC or any other high profile college. Actually I don't even remember the name of her college.'

While waiting for Saba, Yash and I started talking about Audrey and her unconventional style. As we were chuckling, Anjali said, 'Bhaiya, honestly, don't you think I would have been better placed if I were in IIT.'

'No, I don't think so.' The first word 'no' came out from three different sources. One was me, other was Yash and to our surprise the third one was Aditya. The confident reply from Aditya was a spirit lifter. I gestured him to make his point.

'Well......I think....Ahem...See, at a bachelor's level one is not expected to do much of innovative research work. So the most important thing the foreign universities are looking for is your interest in the subject and desire to work further in the field. And if you are clear of what you want to do then I think four years is a good enough time to turn your profile into a 'cannot be rejected' one.'

Astonishment at its pinnacle, we all were looking awestruck at Aditya. We included Yash and Anjali as well as Saba, who was back with the wireless handset.

'Ahem…Audrey online. Audrey here you go on air,' and she put the phone on the loudspeaker.

'Hi Audrey.'

'Hi, Sahil bhaiya, wassup, long time.'

'Yeah right, big shots never thought of giving a call.'

'Oh shut up bugger, as if you have my number on your speed dial'

Getting candid with a bold and beautiful girl on a loudspeaker with people around you is quite a risk and I paid the price for my audacity.

'Someone wants to talk,' and I handed over the handset to Anjali.

'Hi di.'

'Hey, you must be Anjali. Saba told me about you. So, how have you been?'

'I am fine.'

'So you want to do your PhD in Artificial Intelligence from Stanford, right.'

'Ya, and I am too apprehensive about it.'

'And that apprehension is because you couldn't make it to IIT.'

'Yeah.'

'Anjali, I don't know who has put this in your mind but if it is already there, then instead of denying I would rather question it. How do you think IIT can help you?'

'Well….bigger brand…may be,' came out Anjali's nervous reply.

'Okie dear, for a moment let us assume that universities like Stanford do give importance to the brand of the graduate school you belong to. Do you know what the international rankings of IITs are?

Staunch feminist, debating champ, annoyingly confident - Audrey has always been quite aggressive in putting forward her point. Our angelic little Anjali obviously got nervous and could not even reply.

Unperturbed Audrey continued, 'None of them are in top 100 and some are not even in top 200 for that matter. Now even if it is a criterion it obviously cannot be the deciding one in this case. If IITs would have been in top 5 or top 10 then probably that might have made some difference. For professors in top universities of the world IITs are like just other colleges of a developing country. Some of the professors have not even heard about IITs. Your most promising IIT brand is not promising you much, I bet.'

If she would have continued for some more time then probably she would have started abusing IITs and IITians. Anjali was listening to her very carefully and her confusion was clearly visible on her face. She asked, 'Then what are they looking for.'

'Yeah right, they are looking for something else. Now you are talking.'

Audrey is pretty good at doing this. She has her own idiosyncratic style of explaining things. If she would have been a primary teacher she would have probably made nursery students write alphabet A over and over again until they themselves ask for B.

Audrey continued, 'Stanford website clearly states that they are looking for thought leaders. MIT says that passion and motivation are their key lookouts. Princeton stresses a lot on self-learning, experimenting and initiative taking.'

Knowledge and hard work reveal themselves in quite an impressive manner. All sets of ears listening to that were at least impressed.

Incognizant of her admirers Audrey continued, 'there is actually no fixed success hymn but there are a few basic things for sure. The most important being your interest and passion for the subject. A genuine application can easily be differentiated from the pile.'

'How do we make it genuine?' Yash said that almost

spontaneously. Audrey was so impressive that not only Anjali but all the rest of us were also listening to her very attentively.

'And who do we have there...Is that Aditya?'

'No...it's...'

'It's Yash, my friend.' I came to my friends rescue. We both are hopelessly pathetic when it comes to situations like this.

'Oh...hi...Yash bhaiya, How are you?'

'Fine...I am fine.' Yash stammered.

'Sonal di still giving you tough times. I have heard a lot about you guys. Tell her I think she is cool, and by the way jumping out of her hostel at 1:30 am was quite bold.'

My heart skipped a beat and I wouldn't have minded a few more if that could have turned back time. A lot of things happened simultaneously. Yash gave me 'you are a dead man' look, I looked at Saba with surprise and she gestured sorry to Yash. I knew she was pardoned but I was in big trouble.

Few moments of silence probably gave Audrey the hint of the situation and she preferred to continue, 'Coming to the application, you don't have to make it sound genuine, if you are sincere it automatically becomes genuine. Honestly, in four years of B.Tech or should say three years before you send in your applications nobody expects you to do a Nobel prize winning research. You just have to show your interest and display your sincerity and that is more than required.'

I realized that the answer was lacking the objectivity and was more on the subjective side whereas our subject here hates subjectivity and was therefore finding it difficult to comprehend. So I interrupted and said, 'OK Audrey, let us talk about what should Anjali do, step by step so that she gets selected for her PhD in AI after her B.Tech.'

'Stanford', added Anjali spontaneously.

'And please try and answer as objectively as possibly', I added.

'Hmmm...See this is a very clear mindset', said Audrey. 'Students rarely have this clarity at this stage. This makes things quite simpler. If you start now, I would say, that, just 3 hours a week till you send in your application guarantees success with a 99% probability and 5 hours a week would guarantee you a 100% selection in any university on any planet of any galaxy of any damn universe.'

'Sorry!!', came out Anjali's confused voice and we all exchanged confused expressions.

'My apologies, for sounding cryptic. I think it became a little toooooo objective.' We all understood who was responsible for that lengthy "too". 'I meant to say that if you start working consistently now onwards then getting a PhD from the university of your choice in the area of your choice would be a cakewalk. This consistent work would include reading relevant stuff, taking guidance from seniors and professors and staying in touch with the front runners in the field.'

'Di, I am still not able to completely understand that how this all is going to work out.' Anjali said that with a lot of apprehension in her voice. This was quite normal as Yash and I were also not clearly able to comprehend.

'Fine', said Audrey. 'Let me give you a glimpse of your journey forward. If you show perseverance and keep on working in the field of your interest with passion then definitely at the end of the first year you would be qualified enough to get an internship under some professor in the country. After that if you continue likewise and take relevant courses in college then your profile would be able to fetch you a better place in India or abroad for internship. By the end of the third year with the consistent hard work and regular guidance from your seniors and guides you would definitely be in a position to choose your intern in the best universities in the world.'

Audrey continued, 'Now with all these fantastic internship, staggering recommendations and the years of hard work along with the backup of your good grades in college, I doubt even Einstein would deny you a PhD in relativity.'

She was more than impressive and Anjali's spreading lips confirmed it.

Audrey continued, 'So my dear Anjali don't give a damn to whether you were selected in some Joint Entrance Examination of some college named IIT or not; believe in yourself because you are made to do bigger and better things in life and these petty examinations don't make any difference.'

The spread on Anjali's lips was a full grown smile now and she uttered, 'Yeah, thanks.'

'By the way Anjali I have heard that you have a great sense of fashion. We will go out shopping someday. What say Saba?'

God is fair. Yash and I were grinning. It was Saba's turn to get embarrassed.

With that Audrey said goodbye to everybody and Saba went inside with the handset. I bet she would have given Audrey a piece of her mind for revealing so much unnecessary information.

'So miss Mathur, where are we now?' I turned to Anjali.

'I feel a lot better. I did not know about all this stuff. Can I contact her later sometime?'

'Oh yes, definitely, she would be more than happy.' I said in assuring tone.

'You might just take here to some good shopping mall and get her some *a la mode* stuff.' Yash said this mimicking Audrey and we all started laughing.

Saba and Samir came in the living room and mamma also came

with fresh supplies of sandwiches and cold drinks. The mood of the party became light and merry.

After sometime Anjali, Yash, Aditya and I were left in the living room. Yash and Aditya were busy talking about George Solos and his trading techniques. I picked up a magazine and settled in the couch and Anjali was busy thinking about something. She kept on thinking very deeply for some time and then said, 'But Sahil bhaiya.'

'Yes Anjali.' The other two sets of ears also started listening.

'Whatever we discussed sounds very convincing and indeed to an extent I believe in it. But when it comes to practical application is it really that simple?'

'Why would you doubt that? You have yet to experience it.' I asked her.

'I have not experienced it, but have seen it very closely that how difficult it becomes to apply all this.'

'Are you referring to Shweta di?' Aditya said softly.

'Yes'

'Shweta is your elder sister, right.' Yash said spontaneously.

The *'big fat book of what to talk to beautiful girls'* clearly states that you should not reveal any information which is not given by them directly and is collected through any other legitimate/ illegitimate means.

'Yes she is', replied Anjali. Her voice and facial expressions suggested that perhaps she ignored the violation.

'Do you know her? She added softly.

Or maybe she has not. Whosoever violates the rules has to face the consequences. Yash was clueless. The vacuity of his face was redefining the meaning of the word itself. It became worse when Anjali actually started waiting for the answer by looking at him.

'I mentioned her to Yash bhaiya.' Aditya was nothing less than an angel for Yash at that moment.

'So, what were you saying about Shweta?' I tried to take her further away from the *'exceedingly embarrassing situation for my friend.'*

'Bhaiya, Shweta di is doing her engineering from Northern College of Integral Technology. She is exceptionally sincere and hardworking and is among the toppers of her batch. But still she is not happy as the firm she wants to work for doesn't visit her campus for placements. Also she keeps cribbing about the standard of professors and the infrastructure of the college.'

'So what if the company doesn't visit the campus.' I said raising my voice a bit. 'Do you know that on an average only a small fraction of annual recruitment is done directly through campus,' said Yash.

'I don't know who have filled the minds of youngsters with all these crappy myths.' I said this very loudly with an intense feeling of loath for the negativity prevalent in the system and the society as a whole.

Anjali did not speak anything. She looked at Aditya and both of them sat quietly with a guilty look on their face.

'Bha...Bhaiya.' stammered Anjali softly. 'I…I…am sorry…but can I call Shweta di also...Actually I told her and she was interested in coming here.'

'That's absolutely fine Anjali. I will be more than happy if I can be of any help. And I am sorry for shouting. It was not meant for you people.'

'That's fine bhaiya.' Both of them said together.

Anjali took out her pink Nokia N72 and started punching a message. Rest of us got busy into chatting.

I had never met Shweta but have heard quite a deal about her.

She rose to fame when she topped the State Higher Secondary Examination. But ironically her most talked about attribute was something else. Everybody, without exception, thinks that she is one of the most perfect X-X paired homo sapien ever born. Some even regard her as an advanced species which is better in every respect as per the principles of the evolution theory of Darwin.

The random chit chatting went on for some time. Yash, Aditya and Anjali were discussing sun-signs and Yash was explaining the special bonding between Leoneans' and Pisceans.

'Leos are true males and Pisces are true females and together they make a perfect couple'

'Nonsense,' retorted Anjali.

'I am serious; I can give you a million examples of their perfect coupling; right Sahil?'

'Hmmmm....I would say.......NONSENSE,' and we started laughing.

Actually Yash is a Scorpian but a lot of his friends – including me – are Leos and most of them – excluding me – have Pisces girlfriends and they are doing really well. Yash idolizes them as a perfect couple. The second best obviously is Scorpian with Libran; given that Sonal is a Libran.

9

'A' DOES NOT STAND FOR SHWETA THOUGH

There is no substitute for hard work.

–Thomas Alva Edison

Just don't give up trying to do what you really want to do. Where there's love and inspiration, I don't think you can go wrong.

–Ella Fitzgerald

'Ding' went the doorbell and I went to open the door. Black salwar suit; hair till shoulder, few of them guarding the forehead; very small silver earrings and a slick golden watch were adorning her 5 ft 6 inches – without heel – structure. It was Shweta.

'Hi, you must be Shweta.'

'Ya, Hi ….and you are Sahil.'

'So how are you?' I asked.

'I am fine, heard a lot about you from Anjali.'

'Oh, ok, thanks.'

As she was getting introduced to others Saba entered the room.

'Hi, I am Saba.'

'I know. You gave the annual day speech in the school.'

Saba and Shweta belong to the same school – called Study Hall. It is one of its kinds: purely western teaching patterns, no exams, teachers referred as aunties, and all sorts of flamboyance.

Saba was overwhelmed. They shared some nostalgic moments and exchanged some girly courtesy statements before Saba went inside to answer a phone call.

'Di, we were discussing how IIT is not the most important thing in life and how we can get whatever we want even without it,' started Anjali in a spirited tone.

'What we want and how much we want it is more important and clearing or not clearing any examination doesn't make much of a difference in our long term goals,' added Aditya.

Although the look on Shweta's face was enough to say everything but she decided to use words also, 'Huh....I am sorry but I beg to differ. I don't think that not getting into IIT doesn't make any difference. It is huge loss which you carry miserably on your back for the rest of your life.'

For a moment there was silence in the room. Actually nobody was expecting such a blunt response. I was in no mood to let her do this to Aditya and Anjali.

'Hey, I beg to differ.' Yash's tone made it clear that even he was not very pleased by her unwarranted statements.

'I think that's quite an exaggeration. We have been discussing this and we all are convinced that IIT doesn't make any substantial difference', I added.

'Ah haan, prove it please.' That was typical of Shweta (on the basis of secondary information) confidence with a hint of contempt for other person's view.

Among the available options I decided to go for the best one – silence.

'Di,' said Anjali in her stern voice.

'I am sorry. But..,' Shweta made an unwilling effort to cover up for her arrogance.

'No, it's all right.' Yash interrupted Shweta in between. 'I think you have a valid point. And I think it would be better if you make your point rather than we start giving you our reasons.' I was surprised at Yash's boldness, but had major apprehensions about the future course of discussion.

'Why do you think it is that big a deal?' said Yash softly.

'You lose out on a hell lot of things,' replied Shweta curtly.

'Why don't you name a few?'

'Hmmm.... there are a lot of things.'

'Like.'

'Fine...like...., first would be the respect, social value and honor that you get.'

'Don't you think it's immaterial?'

'Hmmm...I do,' replied Shweta and Yash smiled.

Actually for her it was even more immaterial as she would anyway get her deserved social value even if she flunks each and every examination she appears for.

'Alright,' said Shweta, 'I will give you a very practical example. I am in third year engineering and in the coming summers I want to go to some good US university for internship. I know that I would not be able to because: I am not from IIT; I don't have recommendations from any high profile professors under my belt; I have not done any research in the world class labs of IITs; and therefore no one would even bother to open my application form. Whereas my friends who were able to clear IIT will enjoy their summers in the best universities and make big bucks.'

Her eloquence was magnificent but Yash wasn't interested in any sort of appreciation or at least he showed he wasn't. 'Do you think they ask for recommendations for summer internships?' Yash said this in a not so friendly tone.

'Hmmm…I think…I am not sure…I think they do, or else how would they figure out the authenticity of the candidate.' There was a major plunge in the confidence level.

'Well, I am sorry but I beg to differ.' Yash was being ruthless. 'They do not ask any recos at all.'

It was one of the rare occasions when Yash could be seen in such a no nonsense mood. I was enjoying it and just to take a little share of the pie I added softly, 'Yeah, they generally don't and even if they do it is never a deciding factor.'

'Alright, agreed but still you can't deny that it is very easy to get a summer internship for an IITian which they easily convert into an MS or a PhD scholarship or ..'

'Or?' asked Yash curiously.

'Or, just come back with all sorts of fancy shopping, latest mobile, a high-tech laptop, a cool handy-cam and three bags full of chocolates.'

'That's exactly what he did,' murmured Saba softly. I did not understand from where she was appearing every time at the right moment to hit me with her remarks.

'I know,' said Shweta.

For a moment I thought I missed out on something but then I saw the surprise on Saba's and Yash's as well.

'Oh common we live in the same block, isn't it obvious, someone must have mentioned it to me,' said Shweta casually.

It was still not that obvious but it gave me a great feeling which was difficult to hide and to portray that I am normal with it I said, 'Yeah right, I also know that you topped the State Higher Secondary Examination.' That sentence got successfully registered in the list of 'MOST LAME STATEMENTS EVER MADE' in the presence of five witnesses. Why do we do this? Why weren't we taught to behave? I hated my existence.

While I was busy drowning in my self-created ocean of embarrassment. Yash said, 'I don't think that IIT gets to play any important role in fetching you a foreign internship. And trust me it is not simple at all. I mean Sahil sent across around 1500 applications and still could not manage any internship in USA or Europe and had to finally go to Australia.'

I wasn't very pleased to hear all that, but it was actually true. I worked really hard to get my summer intern. Shweta glanced at me and I said, 'Yeah that's true and something which would be even more interesting to you is that my professor Dr. Daniel Cage had never even heard the name of my so called prestigious college before.'

'Why couldn't you make it to the good universities in US; the universities of your choice', said Shweta.

'Ya, valid...especially when they were so ready with the red carpet, to welcome him, because of the great recommendation letter, signed by Ms. Shweta herself.'

Some people never learn. A++ category girls are not very good when it comes to taking sarcasm and Shweta's expression made it quite clear.

'Sorry,' she said in an offended tone.

Before Yash could say anything Anjali started, 'Di.....it is not that simple. IIT is not like up there among the most sought after colleges of the world that the name only is enough to get you everything. Top universities get intern applications from all over the world, the competition is among the best in the world and the so called IIT brand is not that significant at that level and doesn't make much of a difference at a stage of that stature. Actually for that matter no brand makes much of a difference. It's not the quality of the college but the quality and qualification of the student that becomes a deciding factor.'

That was quite a compressed pack of exceedingly impactful sentences. 'I or should say we all agree with her,' said Yash and we all nodded.

All of us except Shweta, and she said, 'Well that sounds a little convincing but still if you go by the numbers then a lot more IIT students get foreign interns as compared to any other college.'

'Very well, maybe, but then they get it not because they are from IIT but because they have worked really hard for it. You see the fancy internships but not the hours of hard work, months of sleepless nights that made them possible,' snapped Yash.

Let me ask you something. 'Where do you want to go for your internship?'

'Any Ivy League', replied Shweta promptly.

'What have you done for it?'

'What can I do for it?'

'Nobody but you can do something.'

'What do you mean? I will apply when the time comes. What else can I do?'

'Have you identified the area in which you want to do your intern?'

'No......not exactly but I would be happy to get something in Artificial Intelligence.'

Don't know what filled the sisters with the lust for the field. Maybe style attracts style; AI sounds quite stylish.

'What all have you done in the field?'

'Well, not much, actually we did not have any course on it yet. But I have read a bit about it here and there and found it interesting. We have an optional course lined up in the next semester on AI.'

'Di, do you really think that this little bit of reading and one semester course is enough to get you an intern in the Ivy League?'

'What else am I suppose to do?' Shweta was getting frustrated on the audacity of her sibling.

But, Anjali was not worried about showing any deference and with all the conviction she continued, 'that's exactly where the problem is. Why are you waiting for a course to increase the knowledge on the subject? You could have read books, talked to learned people of the field and worked with them on some projects. Do you know the top names in AI in the world or in India for that matter?'

'Umm.....No.'

'Are you aware of the recent developments in the field or the major ongoing projects worldwide?'

'Not really...actually...'

Shweta was full defensive and before she could say anything else Anjali blasted, 'then what do you think some angel would descend from heaven with an invitation for your AI internship in Stanford under an erudite professor who wants to work with you just because he is terrifically impressed by your consummate ignorance of the subject or you actually believe in the prediction of Mrs. R.K. Mathur, who happens to be your mom as well, that Shweta Mathur is the chosen one and she would be the leader of the new age AI revolution.'

Yash and I looked at Aditya and he nodded to convey that – *yes I told her that IIM and IIT lake Enara statement used by Yash bhaiya.* She used it really well and she knew it. She looked at us; we gestured appreciation and she smiled.

Shweta did not say anything. It is difficult to tolerate the aweful behaviour of your young-submissive-overshadowed sibling, but the truth was very powerful and had the potential to unfold an unexplored sphere of knowledge and wisdom for her.

I was happy because it would have taken Yash and me quite a lot of extra effort to make her understand the same thing.

'Is it the same for IITians also? Do they also work this hard all round?' Shweta asked in a much lowered tone.

'Yes, it is,' I replied.

'So you worked for three years to get your internship?'

'No, I did not. But then what did I get? I worked on a project of which I did not have any remotest idea and forgot it in entirety before even landing back to Delhi. I essentially wasted or we can say enjoyed my summers as a paid holiday in Australia. And trust me if you also apply to 1500 professors all over the globe at least one of them would definitely pick you up. And as I told you my professor had never heard of IIT before; for him I was just an enthusiastic Indian student with an average CGPA. Do you want to waste your summers in a paid holiday in some stupid country.'

'No I don't. But am I not already very late for having a profile worthy enough of a good intern?'

'Hmmm.....actually no you are not. You have 2.5 months of summers left and then one full semester before applying for your internship. It is enough time and if you utilize it properly you can get whatever you want to.'

'I wish I would get you talk to someone who managed a good internship,' I said thoughtfully.

'I think she is already talking to that someone', said Yash teasingly, 'What say Mr. Fraudie? Mind sharing some experience?'

'Hmm…I don't mind. But firstly, my internship as I said was not that good and secondly, being an IITian I think I am automatically disqualified as the credit of my hard earned internship would go to my far-famed college.'

'Oh yes, I forgot we have an incredibly biased audience,' joked Yash. Anjali and Aditya smiled. 'But I think Gopal could qualify,' added Yash.

10

GOPAL'S GYAN

The only place where success comes before work is in the dictionary.

–Donald Kendall

Being defeated is only a temporary condition; giving up is what makes it permanent.

–Marilyn Savant

Gopal was my fellow intern under Prof. Daniel Cage in Australia. He was also a Chemical Engineer from some college in Kerala. I was envious of him as he used to get AUD 120/week more than me.

'Right, good point. I think I can call him,' I replied.

As I went inside to call Gopal, Saba entered with more supplies of sandwiches and cold-drinks. I came back with the cordless.

'Hey Gopal, I am putting you on loudspeaker.'

'Hello, everybody' said Gopal.

'Hi, Gopal, Yash here.'

'Hey, Yash. How have you been mate?'

'I am great.'

Two things that Gopal brought back from Australia were his trillion dollar watch, which Prof. Cage gifted him, and the Australian accent. Already overflowing with accent being a south Indian he generously adopted Australian style as well. The mixture was an all together new style – definitely not very soothing for ears – of speaking and pronouncing words.

'Yaar, there are quite a few people here interested in listening to how you managed to get your summer internship and what all should be done to get a good internship in ones field of interest?' uttered Yash quickly.

'Ya, Sahil told me that. I don't know how helpful I can be but if you want to know then, I personally developed interest in nanotechnology after my second year in college. In my summers I could not get the opportunity to work with any professor as no one in my college was working on nanotechnology and I had no credentials with which I could have got an internship somewhere else.'

As Gopal mentioned it, I remembered that I did my intern in nanotechnology.

'So what did you do to improve your knowledge on the subject?' asked Aditya curiously. He spoke after quite some time.

Indifferent towards the identity of the questioner, Gopal – with typical gopalness – continued, 'Well I had to spend my second years summers in the college and I spent that in studying about nanotechnology. It was quite a difficult time as there were not many students left in the college and I had no support from any professor.

Although our library had a good collection of books but it was really difficult to choose the starting point.'

Gopal gives the minutest possible details in a very methodical manner. I would not say that is bad but in his case there are no exceptions to this. I feared that he might now come to the names of the books he found out; then the ones he shortlisted and then finally to those he read.

'I started with *'An introduction to nanotechnology'* by *'Kane Douglas'* but I did not find it much interesting so started looking for some other book. I could not find any other suitable book so I thought of taking help from someone senior in the field. I did a lot of net search and posted queries on various online forums. You won't believe that I actually mailed Prof. Henry Marsh of the Melbourne University asking him about which book to start with.'

I wanted to say that I would totally believe him even if he tells that he mailed some professor on Pluto or Uranus asking for something. I realized that I have grossly underestimated his elaborating and detailing abilities and BSNL would definitely make a fortune out of this call if I do not intervene and so I did, 'So that summers you studied nanotech and increased your knowledge on the subject.'

'Yes, as I said,' he replied curtly. Gopal never used to appreciate my interruptions in Australia also. But perhaps the point was conveyed.

'So, what did you do in the next semester and then when did you apply?' I asked quickly.

'Well next semester I was busy with the courses but continued my study on nanotechnology and kept on increasing my knowledge.'

'But wasn't it difficult to do that. I mean given the load of your academics,' asked Shweta.

'Good question, actually it was very difficult and at times it became really frustrating also, as I wasn't getting any support from anywhere; friends, seniors or professors for that matter. But I made it a point that I would, at least devote 20 hours every week to it.'

'When and how did you apply?' asked Aditya.

Gopal definitely did not like it. He wanted to give the comprehensive description of each and every day of his two semesters of hard work and consistent effort but he was helpless in front of our impatient audience.

Reluctantly he decided to give up on the details and said, 'I made a list of professors in good universities who were working in the field and their ongoing projects. I shortlisted 26 professors and applied to 10 in the first round somewhere around October. All were from US and only one of them was courteous enough to reply but that too negative.'

'Then?' asked Aditya impatiently.

'It came to me as a blow. I felt as if all my hard work and sleepless nights were a waste. I got really depressed and for some time I almost gave up the thought of applying. I went to a professor in my college and told him about all this.'

'The professor was very supportive. He listened and empathized with me. Talking to him lifted my spirits and I decided to start all over again. I made a list of 57 professors this time. I also worked on modifying my cover letter and the CV (Curriculum Vitae) to make them more appealing.'

Gopal took a pause, but at this point the audience was way too excited to let him take the liberty of pauses. 'So did anyone reply positively this time,' Shweta asked impatiently.

'Hmmmm.....in a way yes but no as well', replied Gopal.

'What is that suppose to mean?'

Poor Gopal was not aware about the kind of listeners he had on this end and was definitely having a tough time matching the expectations.

'Well, I mean I got positive replies but then they were not ready to sponsor my visit and I was not in a position to afford it so it was not of much use for me.'

'Ok, how much money is required to afford a decent internship in US,' asked Shweta.

'Which year are you in?' It is quite difficult even for a guy like Gopal to avoid a voice of that quality for long.

'Junior year.' Personal questions will be answered tersely (that too if answered) is given on the first page of the *book of dos' and don'ts of talking to beautiful girls.*

'The cost of three months stay and the return tickets generally comes around AUD 3000,' said Gopal.

'So, how did you land in Australia then?' asked Yash.

'Well, I was extremely disappointed after the responses. I knew that I was not in a position to afford that kind of money. I gave up the thought of an internship abroad. It was almost the middle of January and most of the vacancies for summer interns were filled up by that time. Dejection at its peak, I took off from college for a few days and went home to spend some time in solace with my parents and relax.'

Everybody was listening quite interestingly. For the first time I was also enjoying his elaborateness.

He continued, 'I told my dad about how my one year of hard work is getting wasted and I could not do anything about it. He offered me to arrange the money which I happily accepted without even realizing the difficulties he would face in doing that.'

'I was extremely happy. I confirmed to the professor that I would be coming to work with him in the summers and started preparing for my summer intern with full vigour and energy. After spending a good six days at home I was going back. I was very happy and excited and would have remained so if I would have overheard the discussion of my parents about arranging the money for my summer internship.'

'I hope I am not boring you guys.' He has never asked that before and I so wanted to say that for the first time you are not at all boring.

'No,' came out few voices from the audience.

'That moment I realized what a useless sloth I was being. I was not working at my full potential and blaming hard luck for my failure. I charted out a detailed plan to apply in a more efficient manner. I made a list of 396 professors from all over the globe, who were working in the area of nanotechnology. Next, I made properly tailored draft applications for all of them and started sending them as per the pre decided schedule. For the first hundred or so I did not get any positive reply.'

'The first hope came from Germany, Professor Hedley, who asked me to work on an ongoing project with 'Nanotechnology Development Corporation'. He offered me to pay for my airfare and make arrangements for my stay. After that, as if the doors were opened and offers started flooding in; some partly and some fully funded. By the end of February, I had 3 fully funded and 11 partially funded internship offers.'

'Why did you choose Australia then?' came the obvious question from Yash.

'Well I was confused between Prof. Dan, Swinburne University Melbourne and Prof. Alfred Dreggier of West Coast University. I finally decided to go for Australia because of two reasons – one of them was definitely the alignment of the work with my interest.'

'What was the second one?' I asked.

'The second was not that important but I wouldn't say that the kind of money Prof. Dan offered did not tempt me.'

'450 AUD/ week is not that much money.' I replied

'Well, I am sorry but that's what he asked me to tell everybody. He actually promised to pay me 600 AUD/ week. But he couldn't pay me more because of certain project rules he had applied on all other students. So...'

'So?' I said impatiently.

'So, he paid me by other means and made it 600 AUD / week as promised.'

'And what exactly were those means.' I asked shocked.

'Hmmmm......he paid me the executive class Delhi-Melbourne return airfare of the costliest airline, whereas I had taken the cheapest ticket. Then he gave me five times the money required to make that project trip to Sydney.'

I was furious; had no idea of what to say and went out of the room.

I heard him saying, 'So all I want to say is that you just have to keep trying. If you try hard and give it your best shot then it is not that difficult.'

After that Aditya asked a few questions and then Gopal tendered goodbye to all and disconnected.

As I entered the room again Yash started, 'Hey, what the hell is this? What was Mr. Cage thinking? Was he out of his mind or what? How can he treat you like this? 120 AUD less than a peer! Oh no no...actually 120+150.....270 AUD less than a peer. Hey do you think we should file a case against him under the Labour Act of the Federal Government.' Laughing along with the rest of them was my only option.

'I hope that was helpful.' I asked Shweta. She smiled and the rest was understood. Actually Gopal was much more helpful than I thought he would be. He presented a pretty much perfect example of hard work and perseverance.

It was 7:00 in the evening and everybody was in a very light mood. Shweta, Anjali and Aditya looked quite better. Saba was talking to Shweta and it seemed as if they were getting along very well. Mamma entered with 7 bowls of Maggi noodles. We all so needed that. After some more discussions all of them parted .

11

ONE NIGHT FIGHT

Success is how high you bounce when you hit bottom.

–George Smith Patton

The majority of men meet with failure because of their lack of persistence in creating new plans to take the place of those which fail.

–Napoleon Hill

It was just me and Yash sitting in the living room now. We went out for a walk. My society is quite a fantastic place to live; three towers with 4 floors each, a badminton court in between them, a tennis court on one side, an adjacent squash court and a big cricket field. We started walking on the road towards the tennis court. We both were probably analyzing the same thoughts over and over again.

'Yaar do you think it was enough to last for long.' Yash finally gave words to the thoughts.

'No.' I said spontaneously.

'Any ideas?'

'Hmmm...yes but I am not quite sure about it.'

'Let's see what you have got.'

'Yaar I was thinking it was just me and you and a few more people like us who were talking to them....'

'So...'

'So, if we can get them to talk to people who have actually gone through more in life and sitting at higher altitudes and therefore are in a position to give a broader picture of the problem, it would be more helpful.'

'At one point time you say that we need to talk objectively and now you suggest these people who would at the least be super subjective.' Yash was not very pleased with the idea. But somehow I felt that what we did was just the ground work and there is a lot more to be done and we are not even qualified enough to do that.

' Look, I agree, we have explained them things in a very objective and easy to understand manner but I think the effect would not last long if they don't actually see the results. We have to give them, should say, show them, live examples of what we have tried to convey. I want them to see that how successful some of these people have become who were at some point of time standing on the same ground as they are. I think if we make them stand face to face with these icons they can perhaps see the glimpse of the potential they have within and the possibilities life has got to offer.'

'Wow what an idea man', said Yash in an undecipherable tone. 'So these icons, I mean the ones you are referring to, are these the same people whom you met in the Goa Carnival last year.'

'What?' I replied with every bit of surprise in my voice. 'I have never been to the Goa Carnival.'

'Yeah right…neither do you have these supposed icons a phone call away from you…Welcome back to the real world.'

'Very funny, Mr. Bean. But sorry to disappoint, I am serious.'

'Oh you are Sirius…Hey Sirius Black I am Harry Potter...nice to meet you out in the real world...Accio ICONS.'

'Shut up and just.....just vanish you rascal.' I got really pissed off. Yash sensed it well and decided not to irritate me further. I was standing against a wall and he started walking away from me. After taking a few steps he turned and said, 'How do you plan to approach them?'

'I was also thinking about it. We might have to use our entire network.'

'Yes, that is fine. But then don't you think we are looking for quite a bigger set at least in terms of diversity.'

'Why the hell, do we have friends and what for are they working in other companies? We will ask them to fetch more competent people.'

'But still yaar I have my doubts. Anyway when are we planning to do all these interaction sessions as I am going back to Delhi day after tomorrow.'

'So am I.'

'Then?'

'Tomorrow.'

'Are you nuts?'

'Yeah I am. Come let us go.' And I took Yash by his hand and started walking briskly towards home.

'You know what if, I have to choose one alien from all the people

I have ever known, It-would-be-YOU.' Yash said this in a very 'leave me alone you alien' tone as I dragged him along.

'Yeah yeah, I am the alien, come I will show you my spaceship,' and I started moving faster.

For the next few hours we were working on my plan. We were sending emails, making calls, dropping messages at all possible avenues. It gave us the feeling of the one night effort before the final exams also commonly referred to as the *'one night fight'*.

We took dinner in my room and kept on working until 3 am. I could feel the fatigue in my entire body. It was demanding sleep to carry on any further. I dozed off after some time leaving behind Yash who was busy shooting emails and sending text messages. That night we sent more than 100 emails in total.

12

THE DAY AFTER

Success consists of going from failure to failure without loss of enthusiasm.

–Winston Churchill

I can is 100 times more important than IQ.

–Author unknown

'Bhaiya...bhaiya'

'Bhai...Bhai.. Sheena Chachi from USA.' I heard faint voices of Saba and Samir and then felt the weight in my hand. It was the cordless handset and our aunty from US was online. Whenever she calls, her biggest objective is to make sure that she talks to everybody present within the 500 meter radius. And she doesn't really give any respect to anybody's freedom while achieving her goal.

'Hello'

'Hello Shanti baba. My dearest, how are you?'

'I am fine. How are you Chachi?'

'Battu, I am also good. Missing you guys a lot and specially you the most.' This was her second attribute; she gives me new names at the rate of around 5 per minute.

Then she repeated for the trillionth time her visit to our place and how much she enjoyed it. But, how better it is in US and why we all should come and settle there.

As I was struggling to keep up with Sheena Chachi, Yash woke up by the sounds. He straightaway switched on the PC. Sheena Chachi continued but my attention was somewhere else.

'I can't believe it! So many replies! Dude…dude have a look.'

I handed over the phone to Saba and jumped for the computer screen. What I saw was good enough to give me an amazing feeling of accomplishment. We had replies a lot of replies; expected replies and unexpected replies; short replies and larger-than-life ones.

We called up Aditya and asked Saba to call Anjali and Shweta and tell them to come over at 10:00 a.m. It was 9:15 a.m. already. We hurried through our breakfast and straight away went to the living room, along with my laptop.

Aditya was the first one to come and within 5 minutes Anjali and Shweta were also there. After the initial chit-chat came the expected question.

'Bhaiya, I was wondering….that…I mean..,' said Aditya.

'Wondering why did I call all of you?'

'Ah....yes'

'Actually yesterday we were thinking that if we would have been in your place then how much impact would have yesterday's discussion had on us. And….'

'And we think that to make everything , as we discussed yesterday, a little bit more impactful,' Yash interrupted me in between, 'we need to do a little extra effort and to do that effort we have called you people here.'

He continued, 'Yesterday we tried to contact a few people who have made big in their lives so that they can share their idea on the issue with us. We called a few of them, sent mailers to a lot others and tried all other resources to get in touch with as many of them as possible.'

'The effort has not been totally successful but I would say that the results are not disappointing either.' I added.

'We have got replies from some people who have shared their views and ideas and some of them are even ready to interact with us on the issue,' said Yash.

As expected all of them were happy but at the same time the mixed looks on their faces showed that they were still quite apprehensive about the whole scenario.

'Would you guys like to eat or drink anything before we start?' I offered.

'Maybe some sandwiches or cold drinks.' Yash said facetiously. Yash makes a lot of fun of the fact that we serve a lot of cold drinks and sandwiches and blames us for propagating unhealthy eating habits. 'Maybe Shweta would like to have some.' I don't know why he said that. I personally would consider speaking that sentence equivalent to stepping on a landmine.

And it blasted. 'Dude, right now I might deny the best of the nectars offered by the Gods themselves. So please for heaven's sake save your delicious sandwiches and the most tempting cold-drinks for later,' said Shweta cheekily.

Yash looked at me and to avoid anyone else's listening I spoke in the soundless eye language. We do it, we pay; we do again and we pay again; we keep doing and we keep paying; but 'we will never learn' goes the adage. One should try and get this straight in one's head – one should not act smart in front of the combination of GIRL-INTELLIGENT-DROP DEAD GORGEOUS. Yash made a few *I am not guilty* and *she is too rude* appeals, again in eye language, but then compromised with his destiny.

For obvious reasons I had to take it from there. 'Actually we got replies from people of diverse backgrounds and at different stages of their professional career.'

'Okie,' said Anjali cutely. She was probably trying to cover up for Shweta.

I opened the laptop. 'Well the first and the promptest reply came from Akshat. Akshat Pandey is my senior in A&P.'

He was the same guy Saba mentioned yesterday. He is not from IIT but can give any IITian a run for his money. Working with him had been quite a learning experience. As far as A&P is concerned, it stands for Allen & Parkins Pvt. Ltd., a business consulting firm.

'In the mail we told him about the issue and whatever we discussed yesterday and asked for his comments. So here goes the reply –

"Hey,

Quite a mail man! You know how tied up I am but still found it real hard to ignore this one.

The first few currents of feelings while reading your mail were of nostalgia and fear. I went back to the days I was preparing for JEE. How much I sacrificed for it and how pathetic I felt when I could not make it. I was so desperate that I wanted to give it another shot but my parents didn't allow me to.

I remember how difficult it was initially to accept my fortune. After the initial disappointment phase followed an era of hard work

Not clearing JEE was no doubt a setback but I don't really think that I lost out much. I might be wrong as I have limited experience, but personally I don't think it makes much of a difference in the long run.

You have asked how I managed to do good professionally. Well, I don't think I have achieved any laurels yet but so far whatever I have done is mainly because of my strong belief in the tri-principle of success; THOUGHT-HARDWORK-PERSEVERANCE. You have to think high to achieve high, then you have to work hard for it and last and the most important is perseverance even in the most adverse conditions.

I can write forever like this. It would be better to directly talk to these kids if you want. Give me a call anytime tomorrow.

Regards,

Akshat.

There was silence. The mail was impactful and the impact was beautifully portrayed on the countenance of the listeners.

'Can we call him?' Aditya said excitedly.

'Well we definitely will, we will have to. He is my senior out there and I have just three weeks left for the next appraisal. Now even if you back out, I will hire someone else but make sure that Akshat gets to talk and blurt out his nostalgia and all other emotional currents.'

Only Yash understood the reason for the vexed tone. Actually, not many people would be really pleased with the fact that the guy sitting as their senior in office is one and a half years younger to them.

'Don't worry you won't have to hire anyone. I really am looking forward to talk to the gentleman,' said Shweta with a smile on her face.

And now he is getting attention as well!! So you see I have quite a few reasons for not having him in my best books.

'I think first we should go through a few more replies.' Yash said realizing that this would not be the best time for me to give a call to Akshat.

13

STRAIGHT FROM HARVARD

When I was young, I observed that nine out of ten things I did were failures. So I did ten times more work.

–George Bernard Shaw

Effort is only effort when it begins to hurt.

–José Gassett

'This next one is from Faiz.'

Everybody present knew about Faiz. He is my cousin and was also a senior at school. After his graduation from some college in Punjab, he worked for four years and then went to Harvard Business School for his MBA.

The mail goes –

Sahil,

I really don't know why you keep landing into situations like these- people coming to you for advice, you allaying their fears, telling them life is all hunky dory!! You have switched jobs from being a consultant at A&P to a part time counselor to dejected souls or what.

Anyway since you have asked me to put down my thoughts for those who didn't get through IIT – here is some rambling.

Will take a top down approach here – starting from some general high level philosophy.

How successful you are is decided by you and you alone. Your family, your friends, your boss – they can't & shouldn't be deciding what metrics you chose to measure success & failure on. If you chose to quantify your success on the basis of exam results – so be it. And if being called an IITian was such a metric and you could not be – then let me be honest, you FAILED. Accept it!!

The good part however is "failure" and especially failures like these are as ephemeral in their "tangible" impact on life as anything could ever be. It happens to the best of us, to all of us, almost all the time. I will go farther to the extent of saying that whenever you are not doing those earth-shattering amazing things, like "getting into IIT :)" you are in fact failing. If you define success as "having achieved what you initially set out to do" then my dear boy no one would ever have achieved a success rate of more than 1% in his/her life.

Look at your own example. God knows why but misery loves company - people somehow feel better if they get to know that someone around them was/has been/ is as screwed up as they are :). I would list down 10 "important" objectives that you had started with at the some point of time and evaluate how you did on those:

- Clearing IIT-JEE with a rank under 500 – Failed
- Getting a Branch Change after getting into IIT – Failed
- Being in the toppers of your branch - Failed

- Publishing any worthy research paper in any field – Failed
- Winning those Business Plan contests - Failed
- Getting a 10 pointer – Failed
- Getting even a decent CGPA (I know this comes from the bottom of my heart) – Failed
- Getting into MIT right after IIT – Failed
- Getting one of those coveted management jobs – Failed

The only one miniscule, worthless, absolutely trashy achievement that you can boast of is that you somehow managed to fill in the right circles in that answer sheet on the day of the horror called – JEE. That's a success rate of 10% (I can make the stats look worse if you want me to).

Wrap up – everyone fails all the time. So stop whining, pull up your socks up and get moving. Set new goals and try to achieve them. You will probably fail in 99% of those or more – but the remaining 1% is what makes this life worth living.

Ending this note with a few lines borrowed from an obscure source on the net:

'So wash your face away with dirt, it doesn't feel good until it hurts. So take this world and shake it. Come squeeze and suck the day, come carpe diem, baby.'

That one perfectly justified its origin from Harvard Business School. Although it was typical Faiz, but it was typical for me; for the rest of them (including Yash) it was something more than that. It was too heavy – quite a lot of information to assimilate and process. May be it was confusing, or may be enlightening; whatever it was, but it was at the least impactful enough to give a broader perspective and wider diversity to everything it touched. Nobody spoke for a few minutes. They were perhaps introspecting and analyzing everything in the new light. As far as I was concerned I was not listening to this for the first time but then every time I hear all this it has an effect, a strange kind of a feeling, a desire to prove myself, you might call it self-realization – the realization of how much I have already lost, how much I have to achieve and how little time is left to do all this.

'I don't know what to say. For the first time I am feeling how insignificant clearing or not clearing JEE can be.' Shweta said this while still analyzing the words of Faiz.

'JEE is just one of the millions of the tests we have to face throughout our lives. The graph of our lives is drawn on the basis of the result points of all these tests. These points definitely can have different weights but then how much substantial deviation a single point among the millions can bring about in the overall trajectory of the graph.' Yash said that in a very thoughtful manner. Faiz's words had quite an impact on him as well and moreover most of my failures Faiz mentioned apply fairly well on him also.

'Yeah, exactly JEE might be a failure, but as I said earlier, it has negligible effect on your total career graph,' I added gently.

'Yeah I go through at least ten failures in a day when I am not able to stick to my timetable, when I oversleep, when I procrastinate my work, when I talk too much on phone, when I miss the taekwondo class due to sloth and many others,' Shweta said.

'Exactly the same thing happens with me.' I added and looked at Yash.

'Dude, I feel depressed. With me it's much worse if I start counting all these then the number of failures I go through in a day is perhaps more than anyone would experience in a life time.' The look on his face kind of amused the others and Anjali chuckled.

'What happened miss. Don't you feel anything like this ever,' said Yash.

'Hmmm....yes, yes I do. I mean I wanted to be in the merit list but could not. Being the head girl of the school, monitor of my class, topper of my class, play in school basketball team and winning the inter-school debate competition are some of the other shattered dreams.' Coincidently these shattered dreams of the younger sibling were just the few feathers of the success cap of the elder one. Although everybody got the hint but were wise enough not to give a reaction.

'What about you Aditya?' I asked casually to make the atmosphere lighter.

'I.... I haven't really thought about it but I think my list would be pretty much like hers.'

'Okie, too much of depressing talks. Why don't we go through another email please?' Shweta said this and came and sat next to me as I was holding the laptop.

14

MOHIT'S REPLY

Put your heart, mind, intellect and soul even to your smallest acts. This is the secret of success.

–Swami Sivananda

When you get into a tight place and everything goes against you, till it seems as though you could not hang on a minute longer, never give up then, for that is just the place and time that the tide will turn.

–Harriet Beecher Stowe

'The next mail is from Mohit. Mohit Pathak was my school junior and was in his fourth year of engineering. Mohit was a very bright student and did very well in the board exams both at the higher as well as senior secondary levels. But he was a little unfortunate in JEE and could not get through. He missed the math's cutoff by one or two marks. He did not appear again and joined mechanical engineering in some college in Chennai.'

'And a month back he got placed at a package of 16 lacs/annum in one of the most prestigous consulting firm for which most of the IITians are ready to give up their right arm,' Yash added quickly.

Actually, the consulting firm that recruited Mohit is the dream company for most of the IITians, or should say any one in the consulting field, and Yash was desperate to work for it.

I started reading the mail–

'Hi Sahil bhaiya,

What a pleasant surprise. I am doing fine and hope things are great at your end as well.

You have asked me a rather difficult question. I don't know whether I am qualified enough to answer it. But nevertheless I would love to give it a try.

As far as I am concerned, you know, I never took it as a setback and did not even appear for the second time. I don't know how normal it is but I have always believed that one is valued on the basis of one's knowledge. And, I think to gain knowledge one doesn't require the crutches of institute, teachers, environment etc. I don't deny that they might be helpful but at the end it's the motivation and desire that count. The most learned never had the best of the resources.

I agree with you that these kids have not lost anything by not clearing JEE. They might have lost on a few things viz. institute brand, most qualified professors or may be the company of some geeky fellows but I sincerely doubt any significant contribution of any of these in ones learning. And moreover at the same time if they have lost something then they also have gained on a lot of things. I would not like to get into the advantages of not being an IITian or I might sound like an idiot chauvinist.

By the way how is Samir doing? Heard he is in IIT Pawai?

Convey regards to everybody. I would be coming to Lucknow next month. Hope to see you then.

Regards,

Mohit.

We could see the smile on the faces. Before I could say anything Shweta said, 'Can we talk to him before going through the next mail please?'

'I fear that would not be possible as he is in US for some induction programme on behalf of his company.'

'Ohh shit,' said Shweta and made a face which cute girls generally use to get the impossible done from (stupid) guys.

15

RESPONSE FROM AN IAS TOPPER

Gift, like genius, I often think only means an infinite capacity for taking pains.

–Jane Ellice Hopkins

Plough deep while sluggards sleep.

–Benjamin Franklin

We moved on to another mail. It was by Mr. Deepak Kumar Shukla. This was one of the most unexpected replies. Mr. Shukla was my client in one of the projects we were doing with the Government. He was the topper of IAS exam in 1994. He always wanted to be an aerospace engineer from IIT Kanpur. In his first attempt he could not appear because of an injury. He had worked really hard for it and therefore it was a major setback for him. Then he appeared two times but could not clear it. He told me that in his third attempt he actually fainted in the exam hall.

After three failed attempts he had to give up due to family pressure. He was determined to prove himself and decided to become an IAS officer. He gave up his engineering ambitions and took geography and philosophy in his graduation. His hard labour for three years paid; he topped the civil services examination and got the home cadre.

After giving his background to the audience I started reading the mail –

Dear Sahil,

It is nice to see your effort.

These children are disturbed by their failure and this shows that they are concerned for their future. If failure is accompanied by despair then you definitely have reasons to be happy. So, the first step is right; their direction is correct; they just have to keep going.

You know what all I have been through in the beginning of my career. Life wasn't at its smoothest with me and fate had conspired pretty well to nip off all my plans in the bud. At times we feel that life isn't fair with us and we start losing confidence and motivation. Actually the irony is that it's actually at that time when we need them the most.

Anything that we legitimately earn in our life in a given period of time is either through hard work, intellect or luck. Life is an undiscovered equation with multiple constants. There can be universal constants ('UK'), applicable on everybody, as well as individual dependent constants ('K'), which would vary for every individual.

Say a typical equation for anyone could look like-

K1 * (Hard work) + K2 * (Intellect) + K3 * (Luck) + K4 * (Time) + UK1 + UK2 + UK3 + UK4 .... = Desire

Now, the Left hand side should be equal to or more than the Right hand side for the desire to be fulfilled.

Let us take an example,

Let there be a person A. A's desire is a Mercedes convertible.

Case 1: A is Anil Ambani's Grandson. Luck factor plays dominant enough to cover for the whole left hand side. Hence desire fulfilled.

Case 2: A is a middle class person but is really hard-working. A works hard and keeps moving up the ladder and eventually is capable enough to fulfil his desire.

Case 3: A is amazingly intelligent and discovers a cure for hair-fall and becomes a millionaire. This although is a rare phenomenon. Not everybody can be Larry, Sergei or Mark Zackurberg for that matter.

I think I have digressed a bit. In context of these children my point is that at the time of the examination may be their luck was not that favourable and their hard work and intellect were not able to cover up for it entirely; whereas for someone else with similar intellect and may be a little lesser hard work the luck factor played better at that time and he/she was able to get through.

So instead of wasting their time in whining they should gear up for their next desire. And, as it is clearly obvious from the equation that IIT doesn't have any effect or presence for that matter, in the left hand side of the equation, therefore they are once again fairly placed with all the "IITians" for the next desire. And this time they might have a better luck factor. Just that they have to keep their hard work at par with their counterparts in the IITs.

Rather I would say that this time they should not repeat the same mistake again and raise their hard work to such heights that luck couldn't stop them from achieving their desire. Not only this, if they really feel the despair in their failure they should make sure that they set their goals really high and achieve them in such a manner that they make "them (IITians)" go through the same despair which they are experiencing now. These kids haven't lost anything tangible and they should take this situation as an opportunity to prove their mettle, especially to those who are right now dancing on their luck.'

'Rascal. I will...'

Perhaps Aditya unintentionally said that out loud. I stopped reading and everybody started looking at him. Before anyone could speak Anjali said, 'Arpit Dubey, right?'

Aditya was embarrassed for his uncontrolled reaction and could manage only a slight nod. Anjali filled us on this new character; how he was able to make it and what all show offs and attitudes he had been throwing around since then.

I started reading again –

'I know the mail is getting too long but I want to share a few fables which I think are extremely relevant and might prove helpful to these kids.

Story 1:

There was a prosperous kingdom. The king was very kind and benevolent to his subjects. Everyone was rich and happy. One day three farmers came to the king with a request. Their wheat fields did not get proper watering due to inadequate rainfall in their region. The king heard their problem and immediately ordered his men to dig a well each for all three of them. The farmers went back happily.

The location of the first farmer's well was very nice and it was always full of water. He started using its water for watering his fields. He had to do a little extra work but he managed it pretty well and at the end of the year got almost as good harvest as he usually used to get.

The locations of the second and third farmers' wells didn't turn out to be the best. After a few months, the wells started drying up and he had very little water for watering their fields.

The second farmer was very dejected. He went to the king again to complain about his misfortune but the king was gone for a campaign. He felt even more depressed and started cursing his destiny. He started wasting his time in crying on his ill fortune and because of that he couldn't give adequate attention to his field. Because of the lack of motivation he did not even plowed his field properly. Most of the seeds got wasted because of the inadequate plowing. The situation became worse because of the limited supply of water due to his negligence, he did not use the water cautiously and his well went completely dry. At the end of the year the second farmer got a paltry harvest and was forced into abject poverty.

The third farmer was also very upset but instead of getting dejected he decided to face the challenge. He started working harder and using water cautiously. To overcome the water shortage he plowed his land better and used the seeds wisely in the most optimized manner. Also, he used the limited water he had at the most appropriate time and watered his fields uniformly without wasting it. To his surprise, he got an excellent harvest which was almost double his usual harvest.

Everybody in the village was surprised. They went to a learned scholar and told him the discrepancy. He explained that the third farmer had a better crop because; firstly, he plowed his land better that increased the productivity of the land; secondly, he dispersed the seeds properly, which further increased the yield; finally, he used the limited water wisely and did not over water his field. All these factors combined together to give him an excellent harvest.

Moral: Actually the second farmer had sufficient water but he was used to over watering his fields. There are times when we think we are deprived of something, which might hamper our future but in reality our future is only in our hands and depends only on our own hard work. Events which come as a bane might actually be a boon in disguise and help us to come out of our comfort zone.

Story 2:

There was a village named 'Kontent'. The village was located at the banks of the river 'Happiness'. As per the legend the river was blessed by the Goddess of Happiness herself with an infinite supply of fishes. All the villagers were fishermen and it was a very prosperous village.

The fishermen used to fish from morning 8:00 a.m. till afternoon 3:00 p.m. Thereafter they would go to the market to sell their fishes. They would return around 6:00 p.m. and enjoy the time with their family and friends. Also they used to take off on Saturdays and Sundays for partying and merry making. As per the legend this went on for centuries until the birth of a boy called 'Ambi'. Ambi grew up to become a fishermen just like the rest but he was a little different. He was not content but intensely ambitious. He was prosperous like all other fishermen but he wanted more from life.

Driven by his ambition to quench his thirst for more from life Ambi decided to put more effort. He decided to fish for one extra hour from 7:00 a.m. to 3:00 p.m. As a result Ambi used to get more fishes compared to others. His fellow fishermen started making fun of him by saying that he was greedy and what difference one extra hour of fishing would make. They were somewhat correct; although Ambi used to make a little more money but it was not substantial. Ambi was not satisfied. He started fishing from 7:00 a.m. to 4:00 p.m. and then sell his fishes at a price little lower than the market price. In this manner he was able to sell all his fishes in a lesser time. While other fishermen spent three hours Ambi spent only two hours for selling. He started making more money. Other fishermen started treating him with contempt and some even called him a freak. Ambi was getting richer but he wasn't satisfied. He interacted with a few customers and realized that there was a huge demand for fishes on Saturdays and Sundays. He decided to work on Saturdays and Sundays as well. As he used to be the only seller he used to sell the fishes at higher prices. Ambi's wealth started increasing rapidly.

After sometime Ambi had enough money and he decided to buy another boat. He also hired a guy named 'Prole' to do the fishing for him. He used to pay him handsomely and therefore Prole never bothered to buy his own boat and preferred working for Ambi. Ambi was now the clear market leader and started making more profits. He bought more boats. After some time he had a full fleet of fishing boats and a lot of people working for him. His market share became so large that he started influencing the prices substantially. Other fishermen could not match his prices and therefore ended up making lesser money. Ambi was paying handsome salaries to the people working for him therefore some of the fishermen sold their boats and started working for Ambi. This further increased Ambi's dominance and made things worse for the remaining fishermen. Slowly and steadily, over a period of time all the fishermen sold their boats and started working for Ambi.

Ambi became the first king of the village, 'Kontent'.

Moral: It doesn't matter where or with what you start with but what's important is where and with what you want to end; start might not be in your hands but end definitely is up to you to decide. If you want extra you have to put in extra. Initially you might face difficulties and the rewards of extra work might not be that great or might not even be noticeable but if you persist the rewards keep growing. Ambition is the fuel for achieving great things in life.

Well, I think my mail has become too long already and I will stop right here. Do let me know how the children took it.

Regards

Deepak Shukla

Ps: What happened to that mission of your mother? Fill me in with any updates.

The mail ended. It was long, really long but I wanted to read, I was so involved that I wanted to keep reading.

'It can't get simpler.' Aditya broke the silence.

'Yeah, I feel guilty.' Anjali said in a low voice.

I looked at Shweta in anticipation of her comment. She was quiet and not only quiet her eyes were full of water as if she was about to cry. We decided against any interference of any sort.

'Who is this guy again?' Saba asked from the door. 'And is the mission he was referring to is the one I am guessing……'

'Shut up,' I stopped her. 'Too much of useless information there Chotu.'

'I worked with him on a State Project in Chandigarh. He is an IAS officer.'

'Hmmmm…..' She gave some Sabaish expressions and went inside.

The mail gave a lot of pointers for thinking. It was long but the amount of information completely justified the length.

'I did not understand one thing', said Shweta softly. 'Why did the third farmer started working harder?'

'Simple, he wanted to cover up for the lack of water,' replied Anjali promptly.

'But then, why wasn't he working harder before he had this water problem,' asked Shweta.

'He was in his comfort zone and was content with what he had.' Anjali replied with an air of certainty in her voice.

'This actually was a very befitting story.' Yash spoke excitedly.

'Take these farmers as three students preparing for JEE. The first student got through whereas the other two were a little unlucky. The second student got dejected and stopped putting in proper efforts and therefore couldn't do much in his career. The third student on the other hand decided to fight back his hard luck with his hard work. His perseverance paid and he was able to do even better than the first student.'

'Yes, this is precisely what we have been talking about.' I interrupted him. 'And this is exactly what we meant when we said that not getting through might actually turn out to be a blessing. This 'insignificant failure' comes as an eye opener and helps us come out of our sloth and realize our true potential.'

16

GOSH IT'S MY BOSS

For us, there is only the trying. The rest is not our business.

–T.S. Eliot

There are no easy methods of doing difficult things; the method is to close your door, give out that you are not at home, and work.

–Joseph de Maistre

'Should we move onto the next mail?' I asked the meeters.

'Yaar, can we call up Akshat first. It's already 11:30.'

'Yes, that can be done. What say junta?'

Unanimously we decided to call Akshat. I brought the cordless and dialled his mobile number.

'Hello'

'Hi Akshat, Sahil here. How are you Sirjee?'

'I am fine. How are you?'

'No points for guessing the motive of my call.'

'You are too stingy with your precious points.'

'Hehe. Let me quickly introduce you to everybody.'

After a quick introduction session the discussion took the intended course. Shweta was the first one to ask the question.

'Sir, did you feel bad when you could not make it to JEE?'

'Well, yes being a normal mortal I did feel bad, should say really bad about it. And, please don't call me sir yaar.'

'Fine, Akshat. How did you manage to progress so fast professionally?' Shweta definitely was more comfortable with this style of addressing.

'Thanks but I really don't think I have done anything great....yet,' and perhaps so was Akshat.

'Alright, alright... you are modest...now can we talk stuff.'

'Ohh...Sorry lady...lets come straight to business then. Can I get something more specific from your side so that I can avoid any further adjectival allegations?'

'How did you manage to get this job?'

'Applied – got an interview – got selected.'

'What made your resume worth fetching you an interview?'

'Now that's a pertinent question? And I would like to answer that if I am assured anticipatory amnesty for any unwitting slips.'

'O mortal soul, do not doubt our clemency.'

Everyone was enjoying the celestial conversation of two super mortals; everyone, except me, stupid chump, who had put his job in jeopardy.

'As far as my resume is concerned, the only few spikes were – I was among the top ten percent in my batch; I was the only one in the batch to have an internship in IIM Ahmedabad and a paper published on 'Management Consulting'; I was the lead guitarist in the college band.'

'Akshat.....,' Yash interrupted, 'can I ask something?'

'Sure, please go ahead.'

'How did you get the idea of doing an intern in IIM Ahmedabad and then how did you manage to write a paper on Management Consulting.'

'As I mentioned in the mail, I am a strong believer in the tri-principle of thought-hard work-perseverance. So it all started with a thought – a thought of working in a top management consulting firm. It was difficult especially because none of the targeted firms come to our college for recruitment. Then started the hard work – I started reading about the subject and gaining knowledge from all possible sources. This went on for two years. After my second year I tried to get an intern in IIM Lucknow but could not make it. It came as a setback. I don't regret it though, as I later got a very interesting intern in Times of India that summer. In the third year I took elective courses related to management consulting and actually started writing a book on the subject. It never got printed though.'

'Anyways, after the third year I had gained enough knowledge on the subject. I sent intern applications to IIM Ahmedabad and IIM Calcutta. To my surprise I got selected in both the institutes. The intern was a very learning experience and I ended up writing a paper. That was pretty much it.'

'I am sorry but could you be a bit more elaborate. You thought and then you worked hard with perseverance – this is the only takeaway as yet. Can we move into finer details?' Shweta said in her usual style.

'You mean the abstruse domain of my mysterious self.'

'Not bad, Mr. Consultant.'

None of us (I mean none of the remaining us except Shweta obviously) were even close to understand the rationale of this enigmatic chemistry between the two souls in this first meeting that too on electronic media.

'Specificity is the key,' came one more weird statement of Akshat.

'Hmmmm.....why were you so sure that what you are doing was the right thing to do? And...did you have a very good friend circle? Or was there any special senior or guide? I really don't know...what all to ask. You have been through this and that too very recently just start telling anything and everything you think is relevant.'

'Very well...they were quite relevant questions I would say. I will take them one by one. How did I know that what I was doing was right?'

Akshat took a pause. The rest of us were still trying to get a hang of the trajectory of the discussion.

'I don't think that anyone can ever be completely sure about the correctness of what one is doing. The key lies in monitoring your progress, reevaluating your thoughts and actions and adapting them for the better. I had an aim of getting into management consulting but had no clue whatsoever of the path.'

'Talking to you is like sitting in a philosophy class.' There is a thin line between candidness and rudeness. And I thought Shweta just stepped over it but thankfully her celestial partner wasn't offended.

'You are a tough client,' replied Akshat. 'Nevertheless, I will be extremely cautious to avoid any further disappointments Her Ladyship.'

'When I was about to join my college one of my cousins, who also happens to be my guide, gave me a very interesting analysis:

'In any college there is a trend. This trend is a very powerful and at the same time dangerous thing. It has the power to engulf you and put you on a trend line. Trend line has got trend points. Each trend point has got defined coordinates on a multidimensional plane. Trend force unceasingly pushes you towards these trend points on the basis of your performance in the different dimensions. So dear, if your aspirations are not among the trend points of your college's trend line then the first thing is to break free of the trend force. This is easier than you can imagine and the rewards are tempting.'

Akshat took a pause. He was probably giving us time to make sense out of it. I was feeling quite incapable of doing it and was ready to bet my fortune that others would not have understood even the smallest bit of what I got. But then, life is full of surprises.

'And how do we know what is required to break free of the trend force.' For once if it would have been Shweta then it would have made a little sense. Aditya was the last one in the room I expected to decode the mysterious verses.

'Good question. That's what I asked him.'

'Okie...but Akshat I think we have a different question here.' After saying this I looked at the rest of the people.

'Yes....yes I agree', added Yash, 'and the answer is a prerequisite for digging further into the matter.'

'Ya. Do you mind explaining your words of wisdom,' came Shweta's statement.

'Oh I am sorry. That was a little cryptic I agree.'

'Yeah....very little,' said Shweta sarcastically.

Akshat chuckled and replied, 'the cousin who said this is himself a very cryptic person and I have had tough times understanding his words. For you guys it becomes even more difficult to understand because I did not give you the reference in which he said this. Actually, we were discussing about my future aspirations and my bent towards management consulting.'

'He mentioned a few good names in the field of my interest and asked me whether I have heard of them and whether these firms come to my college for recruitment. I had never heard of them and trust me the first time I heard Allen & Parkins, A&P, I thought it has something to do with the printing works or some save-trees kind of campaigns. My unusual contentment with my gross ignorance of my own state of affairs brought out his cryptic self and he gave me the not so trendy trend analysis I just mentioned.

'The point he wanted to convey was that because my college is not among the top tier colleges of the country and none of the top firms in which I aspire to work come for recruitment I should start analyzing my situation. The best students in my college generally get placed in some good IT firms in the country or go for further studies in some decent foreign universities or go for an MBA from some good college. For the past few years none have been able to directly make it to any of the big names in consulting, or some Ivy League or IIM Ahmedabad, at least directly after college. So these places are not the trend points of the trend line of my college. Therefore I will have to make extra efforts to travel that extra mile to fulfil my dreams.'

'According to him not even the best students in my college were giving their best attempts for their career and they were just following the trend set by their seniors and the same is happening in all the colleges of India.'

Akshat took a pause and the sound suggested that he was drinking water. Yash said, 'do you mean to say that in every college the future course of any batch is more or less similar to the senior batch.'

'Yes, that's what pretty much I am trying to say.'

'I don't agree completely with you.'

'Point taken, there are aberration and changes depending on the external factors; market conditions can be one such external factor. If there are fewer jobs available or the salaries are not competitive then more students tend to go for further studies. But there are no major changes. Let me give you an example. Tell me one thing – what do most students aspire to do after their MBA from a premier institute.'

'Well...I think nowadays the most sought after, is a job in Private Equity. What say Sahil?'

'Ahem...Yes definitely. They are the highest paying jobs and one can easily aim to be a millionaire before 30.'

'Now tell me how many IITians would love to work in private equity sector post MBA?'

'Quite a good percentage I should say.' Yash looked at me and I gave him an affirming nod.

'How many do you know from the past 10 batches joined Private Equity directly after college?'

Yash was clueless and so was I. But now I understood the point Akshat was trying to convey. It was brilliant and surpassingly impressive.

'I don't think that I have heard of anyone doing that.' Yash still had no clue of what is about to hit him.

'And what do you think is the reason behind it?'

Akshat was rubbing it in and Yash was not even aware of it or maybe now he was as he said, 'Ok, got your point....hmmmm.'

'Oh man,' said Aditya. The admiring smile on Shweta's face confirmed her understanding. Anjali was the only left out and impatiently said, 'What?'

'Trend,' replied Akshat. Anjali did not reply anything but the rapid flow of thoughts in the encephalon was depicted on her visage. No answer can escape the might of a properly utilized human mind.

'You mean to say that a job in Private Equity is not a trend point of IIT and therefore...'

'Exactly!' Akshat said this in quite a stimulating tone. Everybody was thinking and there was silence for some time.

'So you see IITs are no different just that they have a little higher trend points than some other colleges, and that according to me can be positive as well as negative.'

'How can it be negative, Sir,' said Aditya.

'What's your name again?'

'Aditya.'

'Aditya, these trend points are high and therefore tempting. Because of this students tend to restrict themselves to these points and thus are not able to realize their full potential.'

'How can you say that?' Yash said.

'Well yes I cannot prove it but I can present a few case studies in support of my point. First one is of Anant Singh. He was a trend breaker. He did his JEE coaching from the best institutes in Delhi and was among the top performers of his batch. Everyone was expecting him to secure a rank in the top 100, but due to an accident he could not appear for the exam. Instead of reappearing he joined another college in Delhi. He did this because he strongly believed that his success has nothing to do with the college he attends. He worked hard in his college for four years. He did exceptionally well and straightaway went to Harvard Business School for his Masters in Business Administration. Straight admission to HBS again is not a trend point in any of the IITs. Rajat Gupta and few others are the only exceptions to achieve this feat. Anant probably would not have made it to HBS if he would have been in IIT.'

The listeners were mesmerized. I felt a sudden crave to talk to this guy.

'The second one is of Shobhit Pandey. He was also a trend breaker. He was never bent towards IIT and did not even appear for JEE. He joined some engineering college in Punjab. He was an average student there. When he was in second year his father died in a road accident and his father's business partners took over the business.

The deprivation and miseries of his family transformed him and his entire perspective towards life. He decided to be a rich person. He started working harder and harder. He explored all resources and did all the primary and secondary research to figure out the best strategy to accomplish his objective. He started studying finance. He spent his second year summers as an unpaid intern in a management school in Delhi. Whole of the third year he spent studying finance along with securing good grades. He started working with a professor on stochastic process analysis project. After his third year he went to work with a trader in Wall Street whom he contacted through a networking website. The trader was supposedly impressed by his intelligence and zeal for the subject.

Throughout his fourth year he kept on studying finance and cleared many certifications. He got placed through campus placement in a technology consulting firm but he kept on applying for the job of his liking. His efforts finally paid off and he got a job in the most sought after Private Equity firm of the world. He did really well and if my estimates are not entirely wrong, today he has comfortably got at least 20 million dollar as hard cash if not more. He owns a luxurious penthouse in Manhattan.'

With a little break Akshat added, 'This person Shobhit Pandey also happens to be my above mentioned cryptic cousin.'

It was the story, the teller or the protagonist or a perfect blend of the three but the audience was awed. Spellbound we were looking at each other. That was sooo Akshat. I could feel the similar chill down my spine that the clients' praise and the peers' envy after the superbly dynamic and enigmatically impressive presentations given by Akshat.

Be it project reports, client presentations or appraisal interviews Akshat has always been a supporting mentor to me. Yash was busy exploring himself. He had got quite an answer to his question. When we started the discussions with these kids we never thought that the discussion would turn out to be so enlightening for us.

I could clearly see myself sitting on one of the trend points of my college's trend line; got placed on the seventh day of the placement season, after getting royally rejected in all the other good companies visiting the campus in the first six days. I never applied to any other firm off-campus thereafter and was inadvertently intrinsically content with my exceptionally ordinary achievement.

Shweta and Aditya asked few more questions to Akshat. Shweta discussed her future plans with him and he suggested her to apply in A&P if she plans to go for a career in management consulting. I thanked Akshat for his time and guidance.

This was definitely the most enlightening discussion so far. It started out with helping someone with some motivational talks but these two days seem like a voyage with innumerous explorations and findings. We had spent two days chasing the answer to one question – What if not IIT? After two days of dedicated discussions and involvement of many other individuals – most of them much higher on intellect – we have found an answer. Or have we?

If I try compiling my answer to this putatively significant question then I would really have a hard time to come up with a decent and sensible response. I would rather prefer to answer this question in parallel with another question – What if IIT? If I start analyzing these two questions and make a list of what all is achievable if you have IIT and then make a list of the things among these that can't be achieved if you don't have IIT; then even after deliberate efforts and being totally biased for my alma mater, I don't think I can put anything meaningful in the second list.

After the discussion with Akshat the whole environment was different. The belief system of everybody – including Yash and me – had undergone a paradigm shift. IIT does not make any difference whatsoever in one's life; it's in one's own hands to design one's future; persistent hard work is the key to success; one can get whatever one wants with or without IIT; and other similar things, which used to be philosophical sermons became well accepted facts.

There was a long silence and it would have continued if it wasn't for Saba. Saba entered the living room with six bowls of Maggi noodles.

'Bhaiya will starve you all to death,' and she handed one bowl to Anjali.

We all started having maggi and the atmosphere became very light.

17

THE REST OF THE REPLIES!!

Leaders are made, they are not born. They are made by hard effort, which is the price which all of us must pay to achieve any goal that is worthwhile.

–Vince Lombardi

I've got a theory that if you give 100 percent all of the time, somehow things will work out in the end.

–Larry Bird

Random discussions started. Yash went back to the Pisces-Leo chemistry but this time Shweta was blasting off his statements. Probably the issue was sorted out – the souls (five of us at least) were enlightened.

We went through other mails and all of them talked about the same things more or less.

Professor Venkateshwar from IIT Kanpur, Chemical Engineering wrote that out of the 76 papers, which he has published, only 11 were co-authored by an IIT B.Tech, and rest all were by students from other engineering colleges. This was when most of the students working under him were from IIT Kanpur itself. Himself a product of IIT Kanpur, he thinks that the quality of students coming to IIT is declining every year and blames the selection procedure for the same.

Saurabh Agarwal one of my seniors from school, currently working as an Investment Banker in London, wrote an interesting reply.

Sahil ji,

Kitthe rahte ho yaar tusi. Kabi yaad nai karte. Sab changa.

To answer your mail –

See I can put it in a very crude way. You might not like it but at the stage where I operate right now, your question sounds a little lame. Does the undergraduate degree make any difference? Well, brother if I have last 5-10 years record of a person's performance, which is directly impacting millions of dollars of business for my company, why would I even bother to check his degree. You tell me yourself if you have to promote one of the two, where, one guy has a degree from the world's finest college and the other generated a profit of one million dollar for your company, will you put even the slightest pressure on your neurons before making the decision. Bro, degree is helpful, if at all, for the entry. Once you are out there your performance speaks for you.

I will explain you this with an interesting incident, which happened last year. There were two traders operating for our bank in NYSE last year. One of them– Mark – was MIT alum and then a graduate from Wharton Business School and the other – Sagar – was Delhi University graduate and then an MBA from some not so famous US B-school. Both had the same amount of funds allocated to them for investing in the market. Interestingly, when the year-end bonuses were distributed, our friend mark got USD 100K and Mr. Sagar was basking in the glory of being the highest earner for the bank. To appreciate his outstanding achievement the bank rewarded him with a generous bonus of

USD 10 Million!!!!!!!!!!!!

Let me help you visualize:

– A 20 year old average DU graduate

– Rejected by IIMs and other good Indian B-schools

– Applied to US B-schools

– Graduated at the age of 22 from a tier II B-school

– Started with an average job

– Kept progressing year after year

– At the age of 27 became a trader for a well established investment bank

– At the age of 29 usurped the best people in the field

– And now is a multimillionaire.

So now let us analyze this a bit. What did this guy have?

Graduate Degree from an ordinary college – not a very difficult task to do.

Post graduate degree again from an ordinary college – again not very difficult to do.

And still he ended up with millions that not even 0.1% of the IIT or IIM grads earn at his age.

I hope you have got the point here, brother.

Nevertheless, I will give you one more example. There was this friend of mine, my next door neighbour, Suhas. He was my classmate also.

Suhas was a very eccentric person. He was never great in studies but was very intelligent. He was popular, or should say notorious in school for his wondrous deeds, which included:

breaking the desks and chairs of the classroom and burning them to keep himself and a group of friends warm on a January morning extra class, when the teacher was two hours late;

mimicking the school principal on mike in front of the entire school while compering in the morning assembly of his class;

asking his English teacher, a beautiful lady in her twenties, for a date because "he thinks" age should not be a barrier and "10 years" is not that big a difference anyway;

kissing a girl in front of the whole class and many more similar endeavours.

I am sorry for digressing so much from the topic but it was just to give a little bit idea of Suhas.

Suhas and the school continued with each other until he was in standard eleventh, when he finally decided that this place was not really worthy enough to give up the morning sleep every day.

Today Suhas owns Suhas Solutions limited – IT solution firm – with 5000 employees working under him. How he did all that is also an interesting story but I will tell you some other time.

So my dear friend it is not your college, which earns for you. You have to earn it yourself. So make the best of yourself and go make the money. There is a lot out there.

The richest person on a planet once said,

"Money is not the most important thing but make sure you have earned enough before talking such nonsense."

Adios

Saurabh.

That mail was aggressive, crude, and a little contemptuous but then it kind of touched the heart of the problem. Money in a lot of cases, if not all, is an important factor. Engineers are leaving their profession and doing MBA just to earn bigger bucks.

'How much money has this guy got?'

'I don't know Miss Shweta! But definitely a couple of times more than mine and Sahil's taken together.'

'How much money have you got?'

'Ah…Ahem…'

That could have been avoided by a straight and simple answer. But we have promised our humiliated souls that we will keep doing it.

'I am sorry. Just kidding! But I am really surprised by this mail.'

'Yes, it is indeed surprising,' I added.

'Is it possible to work for Investment Banks without a degree from a good college?' Aditya said softly.

'Well yes definitely! Saurabh himself is an example.'

'What has he done?' Anjali spoke after a long time.

'He did his engineering from Mysore and then cleared CFA. For some time he worked with an investment bank in India for its back-end operations and then moved to London after clearing all three levels of CFA.'

'What is CFA?' asked Shweta promptly.

'CFA – Chartered Financial Analyst – is a certification in finance given by CFA Institute of USA.'

'And..' said Shweta.

'What?' I replied.

'Did he get into investment banking just because of some certification from some obscure institute?'

'Miss it is obscure for you because of your limited ambit of knowledge. People who matter are very much aware of the CFA institute.' Yash probably had had enough of her arrogance.

'I am sorry Yash bhaiya. Actually there is such a high flux of spic-and-span information that my cognitive processes are getting a little uncontrolled. I am really sorry.'

If she would have said sorry one more time Yash would have definitely displayed some uncontrolled cognitive process. To my relief he just said it is alright. Understanding the volatility of the situation and to avoid any further risks of conflicts I stepped in.

'See CFA is a reputed certification. It has three levels and only after clearing all the three levels and working in the relevant field for a few years one gets the certification. A lot of students in the senior year of graduation, who are interested in finance, appear for the same. You can check out further details on the web.'

'I feel horrible. I am in my third year and I am not even aware of such important things happening around and I am blaming the world.'

'If it helps even I was not aware,' added Yash, softly.

Shweta gave him a smile which he returned nicely and they both started laughing. It was their sheepish expressions or something else but we all joined in the laughter therapy.

Saba entered the living room and asked all of us to come for lunch.

'Shweta was there any point wasting your one more precious

day with our self-proclaimed counsellors?'

'Hehe....Well, I think they are catching up.'

'Yah…True!!! Catching up… Look who is talking. Ohh my God… I don't know about CFA. How ignorant am I? How dumb am I? Where am I? What all is happening around the world. Someone please tell me nah... Please please….' Anjali had definitely crossed the line there (or should say in the words of Joey Tribbiani (friends) the line was a dot to her).

Even the wildest stretch of our imagination would not have allowed this visualization that just actually took place infront of us. Shweta looked at Anjali, but before she could say anything something else grabbed our attention, a window popped up on the laptop screen – 'You Have Got Mail'.

As I went back to check it Yash said, 'Leave it. Let us have lunch. I don't think there is anything new left anyways for this mail to say.'

I was coming back when my glance caught the sender's name. The Adrenalin rush to my brain was probably visible even with naked eyes as I jumped towards the laptop.

'Hey… Hey...What happened Jonty Rhodes? Has Bill also replied?' said Yash

'Who is Bill?' said Saba.

'Bill Gates!!' asked Aditya.

'What!!!! Bill Gates has replied. You sent a mail to Bill Gates?' said Shweta aghast.

There was pandemonium for some time.

'Shut up! Shut up!' I shouted.

'It is not Bill Gates and neither did we send any mail to him. The mail is from Bharti Roy.'

'Bharti Roy is the Executive Director of my firm. She is like a legend. She was there in the list of most powerful women in the country. I can't believe she replied.'

While I was busy touting my Executive Director, Yash started reading her mail.

Dear Sahil,

If I am not wrong we have worked together on the Brunei's e-Governance Strategy.'

My spirits went to the seventh heaven. I had reasons – firstly, she could place me and secondly, she said we worked "together". So what if I was doing the backend secondary research on my laptop sitting in the secluded corner of the office and she was flying Emirates first class for a meeting with the Prince of Brunei; technically we both were working on the same project.

'At first I did not reply to your mail because I found the subject quite insignificant and a little silly. Later today I was sitting with a friend and I casually mentioned your mail to him. It was while discussing that with him I realized that your mail actually touches a very crucial problem that almost all of us – especially in India – face in our lives and suffer multitudinous losses because of it.'

'I do not want to sound demanding but if you want you can give me a call I would like to talk to these kids. So if it is not a problem please call me at your convenience at the number given below . I am in Lucknow for a project meeting otherwise I would have requested you to come to my office. What a demanding lady, you must be thinking!!!

I will wait for your call then.

Thanks and regards

Bharti.

It was closer to a dream than reality and I would have denied it if only one sense organ was involved. But I was hearing and reading at the same time. The mail shook me from my very core. She is waiting for my call and she is in Lucknow. For sometime I was just hearing voices around me but could not make any sense out of them. It seemed as if I was stargazing. Flabbergasted-perplexed-overawed I picked up the handset and dialled a number.

'Hello.'

'Hey Akshat. Sahil here.'

'Hey buddy. What happened? Miss Shweta still has some questions left?'

'Bharti mailed she wants me to call her.'

'Who Bharti?'

'Bharti R...'

'Bharti Roy!!!!!! Are you kidding me? You mailed her!!!! She mailed you back!!!! She asked you to call her!!! What???...How??....why??

Akshat went on with his extreme exclamations and finding it impossible to hold back my excitement I also joined him. We were at our highest pitch for the next few minutes and a note higher would have made the requirement of telephone unnecessary. When our electrons came back to their normal orbits I said, 'So should I call her?'

'Yeah...well...let me think...it's a tough one. JUST CALL HER DUDE. SHE HAS ASKED YOU TO CALL HER. I don't see you are left with an option here.'

Varying wavelength of Akshat's voice was making it difficult for me to fix the distance of the handset from my ear. Akshat and I discussed my opening lines for some more time and then he wished me all the best for the call and asked me to keep him posted.

'Are you Ok now?' asked Shweta.

'Not really. You carry on for lunch I have to call BHARTI.'

'Do you have a crush on her?'

'Huh!!..What?'

'I mean you know. She is this incredibly dynamic, charismatic and powerful lady. It is quite possible for a young executive to have a crush on her.'

For a moment I was petrified. I was looking at Shweta and everybody else was looking at me. Probably I was actually thinking - Do I have a crush on her? But very soon I was back to normal and snapped, 'Miss Shweta and her Shwetonic Nonsense.'

'Carry on people. Please carry on for lunch you buggers and leave me alone with this living room and this handset.'

Tring Tring!! (5 times)

'Bharti Roy'

'Hello Maam!!. This is Sahil. I got your.......mail.' I was using every bit of my calorie reserve to control anxiety and all related feelings in any sort or form.

'Oh yes! Sahil!! Glad you called. Thought you won't.'

'Yes that was a possibility. But only if I would have died out of excitement after reading your mail.'

Why I said that would be a research question for human psychologists for ages.

'Hahaha. Thank you I will take that as a compliment. So where are the kids?'

'Maam...actually they..'

'You can call me Bharti.'

'Ahem...Oh ok! Bharti actually we all are in Lucknow as well. Actually I just completed a project and had taken leave as I...'

'Ohh that's great. Why don't you guys come over then? I mean if that's not an issue. 5:00 p.m. Taj Palace room number 208. Tell me if it is OK.'

'No I think 5:00 p.m. would be fine. We will be there.'

I said that one with a lot of confidence. I liked myself for that for a long time.

'See you then.'

'Sure.'

'Bye then.'

'Bye.'

18

BHARTI ROY

> Hard work certainly goes a long way. These days a lot of people work hard, so you have to make sure you work even harder and really dedicate yourself to what you are doing and setting out to achieve.
>
> –Lakshmi Mittal

> Patience, persistence and perspiration make an unbeatable combination for success.
>
> –Napoleon Hill

We planned to leave at 4:30 pm. Taj Hotel is just a 15 minutes drive from my house. Saba also requested to come along. Shweta, Anjali and Aditya went to their houses to get dressed for the meeting and Yash and I started exploring my wardrobe; Saba as expected did not find it necessary to change. The rest of us were in the living room, at 4:15, decked in our most appropriate clothes.

Yash and I were in formal shirt and trousers and so was Aditya. Anjali was looking cute in her jeans and top. Shweta was a definite show stealer – with a black designer salwar suit, a matching bracelet, a slick silver colored watch, a two-inch high footwear, a mesmerizing perfume and a mind blowing hairstyle.

We left at exactly 4:25 pm; one black Santro – with Yash, Shweta, Aditya and me; and a kinetic Honda – with Saba and Anjali.

We reached Taj at 4:45 pm. Our entry got a lot of attention as Santro is quite an aberration to the catalogue of cars entering the Taj Hotel and Saba's Kinetic was definitely among the selected few of its clan to leave its tyre-prints on the corridor of Taj.

After parking our vehicles we straight away went to the reception. For a moment I thought we should wait for 15 minutes and go to Bharti's room only at 5:00 pm; but I was late. All six of us had made confident progress towards the receptionist and that had already got her attention. It just spontaneously came out of my mouth,

'We are here to meet Ms. Bharti Roy.'

'You must be Mr. Sahil.'

It was my first experience of being recognized by name by a 5-star hotel receptionist. Ego balloon at its elastic limit I smiled and nodded.

To our surprise she – the 5'11" stunning receptionist, with a British Accent – herself escorted us to Bharti's room – The Presidential Suite of the Taj Palace Hotel.

'So now I know why our clients are so happy with us – our consultants are very punctual.'

'Welcome Sahil and the rest of you. I am Bharti Roy and I work for A&P. Please make yourself comfortable and can we have a quick introduction please?'

'Hello mam! I am Yash. I am working as an Associate in Boston Analytics Group.'

'Hello Yash! I hope your firm is not a competitor in any of our sectors of operation or my folks at A&P would sue me.'

'No maam, we are into analytics only,' replied Yash smilingly.

'Great, then probably you can be our client.' Bharti chuckled and turned towards Anjali.

'Hello maam! I am Anjali. I am giving my engineering entrance exams.'

'Hello Anjali, really nice name.'

Hello maam! I am Aditya. I am also giving my engineering entrance exams.'

'Hello Aditya.'

'Hi! I am Shweta.'

'Hello.'

Bharti turned to Saba. 'Ohh hi, I am Saba, Sahil's sister.'

What a stupid introduction I thought to myself and looked at Yash whose expressions seconded my thought. Bharti's reply confirmed it.

'Yes! I understand that's quite an engagement in itself.'

Saba does not like replies of this kind and she makes it clear. I was praying to the Almighty to save me from bursting into flames and for a moment I thought that my prayer was heard, but then,

'I am in my final year B.Arch. I thought it is away from the conventional stuff and a little out of context so did not mention.'

'Great!! Architects are quite an impressive creed. In one of our assignments we were giving consultancy to the federal government of a country for making a replica of White House. There I got to meet a lot of architects from all over the world. It was a fantastic learning experience.'

Those who knew Saba could make out from her expressions that she was impressed.

Two waiters entered with trolleys of fruits cakes, pastries, soft drinks and juices. Candid discussions started and after some time when we all were a little comfortable Bharti said, 'So where were we?'

I don't know how I did that but I narrated to her the happenings of last two days in around two minutes.

She thought for a moment and then said, 'So who all are convinced that what if not IIT, it does not make any difference.'

All of us made affirmative sounds.

'I am sorry but can you raise your hands please.'

Six hands rose; one each of all six of us.

'Hmm… So all of you are 100% convinced that IIT does not make any difference what so ever.'

Three hands went down – Anjali's, Aditya's and Shweta's.

In consulting that's called 'reality check' and our Managers and Directors are incredibly good at doing that.

Eyes wide open – the remaining three of us took our hand down with surprise and confusion.

Bharti looked at the three of them, smiled and said, '14 years back I was in exactly the same place where three of you are right now.'

She continued in a thoughtful tone, 'I can clearly remember the day when the results came out for IITJEE. That time there were only five of them. My brother, who was a second year student of computer science at IIT Kanpur, came running in with the newspaper. We checked for my roll number but it was not there. A dream was shattered. My father had already made it clear that he would not allow me to waste another year for any stupid exam, and that, I should change my priorities and focus on things that matter for a girl.'

Bharti was silent for some time. She was probably deep in her nostalgia. But our audience was merciless.

'Then? Which engineering college did you join?' asked Shweta.

'Well, none.'

'None!!'

'My father said that there was no point wasting four years in graduation when the same could be done in three years. So I joined B.Sc. in a college in Calcutta.'

Bharti picked up a glass of juice and continued, 'Next three years was the worst period of my life. Every day I used to blame myself for my miserable state just to make it even more miserable. From a chirpy teenager I turned into a morbid person. Even today the memories of that period give me a bloodcurdling feeling.'

'Then?' asked Shweta. Bharti was probably facing the most impatient client of her life.

'Then, seeing me in such a miserable state my brother who was working in Delhi took me with him. My depression continued for the first two months in Delhi. But then regular motivation by my brother and interaction with a lot of his successful friends and colleagues made me feel that there is still a little hope left. I filled up the CAT form. I prepared really hard for next 5 months. My efforts paid off and I got call from all the IIMs.'

'Wow!!,' said Shweta. There were a few more exclamatory sounds but not very decipherable.

'I prepared for my interviews and got final calls from IIM Ahmedabad and IIM Calcutta. I joined IIM Ahmedabad.'

'From there my life took a different turn. It was like my life had offered me a second chance and I wanted to make the maximum out of it. And I did; I topped my batch.'

'Then?'

'Well from there the journey was pretty simple. I got quite a few job offers, domestic as well as international. I preferred to live in India. Then a few job hops and industry changes and here I am today – working for A&P.'

'So that is my about me. I am sorry I digressed a bit.'

'Not at all maam!! It was a superbly inspiring story,' said Anjali softly.

'Thank you dear. But I can assure you that this story was no special. It does not have any extraordinary achievement or the involvement of any supernatural talent or any miraculous serendipity. This is an ordinary story of an ordinary girl who got rejected in an engineering entrance exam twice – even after putting her best efforts. Any other ordinary girl can have a similar story.'

'You mean to say any girl can do what you did,' interrupted Shweta.

'Precisely.'

'Sorry maam!! But there aren't many precedents'.'

'I agree. So what does that mean?'

'Sorry. I did not get it?'

Shweta did not have a clue, nor did the rest of them, but I understood what was happening there. A faint smile appeared on my face. Bharti looked at me, smiled, and gestured me to be quiet.

'Well, you said that there are not many precedents. I perfectly agree with that. But I maintain my stand that it is an ordinary story of an ordinary girl. So what does that mean? Why aren't there many precedents of the same?'

'Well I don't know maam.' Shweta actually had no idea.

'I don't think it is that difficult a question. There must be some obvious reason of why didn't many other ordinary girls were able do it.'

'May be they did not try to do it,' said Anjali softly.

'Exactly dear!! Exactly! A lot of other girls who could have achieved the same did not just because they didn't try for it.'

There was still a confused look on the faces of the audience.

Bharti continued, 'Any ordinary girl who would have studied for 12 hours a day for 5 months would have cracked the CAT exam. If she would have continued that for the next two years in IIM Ahmedabad she would be among the toppers. Being in the toppers in the topmost B-school of the country she would have definitely got the best of the best job offers. And if she would have continued that for the next 8 years she would be pretty much in the same place where I presently am.'

The countenances were suggesting that the audience was able to understand a little bit now.

Bharti continued in her flair, 'I have not done any outstanding, earth shaking things like writing a new theorem, making a multimillion dollar motion picture, creating a billion dollar company or doing a trillion dollar discovery. The achievements – if at all – I have are the most ordinary and the most achievable.'

'Conclusion: what I have achieved is very easy and achievable. So you see it boils down to how much you want it. Before you get carried away, trust me putting in 12 hours a day for years together is not that easy. You compromise something to achieve something else. It is a choice which always lies with you.'

The smile on the countenances suggested that the audience was fully enlightened. Bharti looked at me and smiled.

Everybody – including me – went in a state of profound rumination. One of the most successful ladies of the country had just proved that her achievements are ordinary and any other girl on the street can achieve the same.

How can it be possible? If it is that easy why aren't other people trying to do that? If it is true then can I become like her if I put in that much effort? These were some of the questions which were popping in my head and probably in others heads as well. I somehow did not have the courage to ask.

'It seems like I have given you a difficult polynomial to solve. I am sorry if I overloaded you guys with information.'

'No maam it is not that. But do you mean to say that any girl who is putting in twelve hours a day would become another Bharti Roy! In a highly competitive country like India it is a little unlikely to believe that people are not putting 12 hours of efforts. I am sure that there would be a good enough number of people who are putting that much effort every day.' Shweta's tone had a little bit of soreness.

Thankfully Bharti ignored it. 'Does anyone else also have this question?'

She did not ask us to but all of us automatically raised our hands.

'Very well! Let me tell you a story. At times stories are more helpful than simple words.'

'Long long ago when there were more interactions between the mortals and the immortals, there was a boy by the name Kripa. He used to study in the school of a very famous ancient saint. Kripa was a sincere pupil and used to study hard. But even after all his hard work he was an average student of the school. Every year he used to put in his best efforts but could only be an average performer in studies as well as sports. Kripa's earnest desire was to go to heaven after death and therefore he was a very obedient pupil and was extremely nice to his fellow mates.'

'Once the saint decided to organize a grand tournament in which he invited the Gods also. The tournament had many rounds for testing the physical and mental skills of the competitors. The winner of the same would be crowned as the Ultimate Champion. Kripa also participated and as always performed average. There was a very close competition between the two favourite pupils – Arjun and Karan – but finally Karan came out victorious to become the Ultimate Champion. The Gods were very happy to see the performance of the pupils and decided to reward them. They said, 'We are overwhelmed with pleasure to see such a perfect display of skills and therefore we will attend this event next year as well. Also, the Ultimate Champion of next year would be given a place in heaven.'

Next year also the Gods descended for the Grand Tournament. This year the competition was expected to be much fiercer as everybody had prepared very hard for it. Some were thinking that Karan would win again while others were supporting Arjun. The competition was fierce as expected but to everybody's surprise the winner was neither Karan nor Arjun. Kripa became the Ultimate Champion. Not only everybody else, but Kripa himself was surprised at this.

Enthralled and surprised at his unexpected performance Kripa went to the saint. 'Master, how did I win this tournament? I have always been an average performer.'

The Saint replied, 'Kripa my child before I answer your question will you tell me one thing. Did you want to win this tournament?'

Kripa replied instantly, 'Yes of course! But last year also I wanted to win.'

The Saint smiled and said, 'Ok then tell me what is that which you desire the most?'

Kripa got a little confused and said, 'Master I have a few very deep worldly desires but my deepest desire is to go to heaven after this mortal life.'

The master smiled. Kripa had the most bewildered look on his face but the master just kept smiling.

'So this was the story of Kripa,' said Bharti and looked at us. We all were also having a pretty much bewildered look on our faces.

'So.' Shweta's "So" sounded like as if it was an acronym for "Cryptic-Lady-You-Don't-Make-Any-Sense."

My heart missed a beat. Bharti smiled.

'So what sense did Kripa made out of that smile,' added Shweta with a weird expression.

Bharti kept smiling and my heartbeat was rising.

'Can anyone tell me what sense it makes,' said Bharti.

I had no clue neither did anyone else.

Bharti waited for few moments and said, 'Well Kripa was an average student because his utmost desire was not to become a good student but to go to heaven.'

'Sometimes the mind knows that something is good for you but then the deepest desires in your heart are something else. Kripa's mind wanted to perform well but his heart desired something else. When the heart's desire got linked with that of the mind's, Kripa's performance improved remarkably and he won the tournament.'

This was the magic of Bharti. Last two sentences enlightened us on the last twenty minutes of talk.

Bharti continued, 'So the best way is to make a connect. Link the deepest desires in your heart with those of your mind and you will get them.'

'Did you make this connect?'

Bharti looked at the questioner. Anjali got nervous and said, 'I am sorry if that was personal.'

'No problem sweetheart. I was anyways coming to that. But, I am happy that you asked it means my words are making at least some sense to you all.'

'For me my heart's utmost desire was to prove myself to my dad. One way of doing that was to become extremely successful in life. That was my "connect".'

I don't exactly remember how long the silence continued after this. We all were busy understanding the sentences of Bharti and trying to make various connections. Bharti probably went into nostalgia.

"Tring Tring"

Bharti picked up the phone and had a very quick conversation with someone and in the end she said, 'Fine see you in ten minutes then.'

Bharti looked at us and said, 'That was Nandini Sahni, my friend. She would be coming here in 10 minutes.'

For a moment I thought that she is indirectly asking us to leave. Probably my stupidity made my thoughts evident on my face; Bharti looked at me, smiled and said, 'I have called her to further discuss on this issue only.'

Then she gave us a quick introduction of Nandini.

'Nandini is a graduate from London Business School. She worked with A&P for some time and then went overseas to pursue other opportunities. We have worked together on many assignments.'

'So was she your junior.'

What kind of question was that? But then Yash was quite for much longer than his normal capacity of not speaking.

'She was a colleague?' replied Bharti.

'How old is she?' asked Anjali.

Oh dear lord why have all of them lost it together.

Bharti looked at Anjali and said, 'I don't really know but she should be somewhere around my age.'

'Her appearance might be deceptive though,' she added with a smile.

Bharti went to the washroom and random chit-chat started.

'She is a crazy lady. I am feeling like killing someone.'

Shweta gave an "I disagree" look to Yash and said, 'No yaar I don't think so. I think she is amazing.'

'She definitely is.' Saba made her existence felt after a long time.

'No doubt,' added Aditya.

'Is she single?'

I looked at Yash and for a few seconds and attempted to burn him with my gaze. When it didn't work I said, 'shut up you Ra....'

Bharti came out of the washroom and at the same time the door bell rang and a lady entered.

19

NANDINI SAHNI

Many people think they want things, but they don't really have the strength, the discipline. They are weak. I believe that you get what you want if you want it badly enough.

–Sophia Loren

There is no point at which you can say, "Well, I'm successful now. I might as well take a nap."

–Carrie Fisher

The fragrance of Chanel filled the presidential suite; black long silky hair were dancing freely around her forehead; black designer sari probably was the reason of the dilated pupils of Anjali, Shweta and Saba; and a Louis Vuitton bag was adding on to her already mesmerizing persona.

'Dude is SHE single,' Yash murmured in my ear.

Meeting such impressive personalities in real life was not an everyday event for any of us. We all were still busy in contemplating and appreciating her for various reasons, when Bharti said, 'Whoa....someone is busy partying!'

'Not really....he took me out for surprise lunch. He came all the way from Delhi for this.'

'You could have asked Mr. Sahni to spare a few minutes to meet your poor friend.'

'Actually he has this meeting with some stupid minister at 6:00 pm today so he had to rush.'

'Ohh...I am sorry...she is Nandini Sahni...my friend.' Bharti introduced her and looked at us.

All of us introduced ourselves. Bharti gave us a quick introduction of Nandini.

'Nandini has worked for many multinational big firms including A&P and is currently heading the Asia-Pacific marketing division of Sony. Her husband, my classmate from school, is the founder and CEO of JR Sahni group of Industries.'

Her personality itself was enough to give us goosebumps and butterflies; this introduction took things to an entirely new level. Some of us made stupid gestures, some made sounds and some did both.

'What!!!!!!!,' said Aditya with the most freakishly bewildered expression. 'So I was right in thinking that Mr. Sahni came in his jet to meet you for lunch.'

All of us looked at Aditya.

'Otherwise how would he be able to meet the stupid minister,' he tried to explain himself.

When we still kept looking at him he realized that his overexcitement was blatantly visible and apologized.

Everybody started laughing.

Bharti started filling up Nandini on the situation. Talking to each other they went outside in the corridor.

Aditya looked at me and said, 'Sorry bhaiya.'

'That's okay yaar.' I took a pause for a moment and said, 'THAT-MAN-TOOK-A-JET to have lunch with his wife. If you wouldn't have done that then I would have.'

'But what world is this yaar?' Saba was overawed.

'Seriously,' added Anjali.

We continued chatting and after around 10 minutes Bharti and Nandini entered the room.

'These branded colleges have quite a following I see. Personally I never realized this,' said Nandini.

'It's built-in in our society maam.'

'No Yash, I come from the same society. I don't think so.'

Yash turned red and went into eternal silence.

'But maam that is true for our country. People do get affected by brands,' added Shweta.

'I am surprised to hear this. I am a graduate from an ordinary college; my husband is a B-school drop-out. I don't think your college brand has any role at all in building your future. At a personal level you might feel good about the brand of your college but when it comes to practical things I don't think it matters at all.'

She took a pause and added, 'At the end it all boils down to Dollars and Cents my friends.'

'What say Shweta?' Nandini turned to Shweta.

Before she could recollect herself to answer, Nandini added, 'Very nice suit, by the way.'

'Oh....thanks maam.' I had never seen Shweta that nervous.

'Look, I understand at your stage it is a big thing. A good college is all that a student desires. But then this desire is as insignificant in the long run, as that of 5 year old child's desire for a toy.'

She looked at our stupefied faces and smiled, 'OK may be not as insignificant but almost.'

'Steve Jobs, Dhirubhai, Sam Walton – none have the best of the education or resources when they started.'

'We are sitting in this room talking about studying in some college, which is considered good. I am sure there are rooms where people are discussing about building a college ten times better than the one we are discussing here.'

Nandini took a pause and picked up a glass of juice.

She continued, 'We are talking about getting a degree from some college, whereas, there are people whom the best colleges are dying to confer honorary degree but they don't even bother to come and collect it.'

'The game out there is much bigger my friends and the people who are winning it are very much like you and me. The rules are simple. You get what you want; you just have to want it enough.'

Spellbound we all kept listening to Nandini. It was more of a monologue. She was giving us examples: of people who started off in their thirties with a below average career to become multi-millionaires; of people who were drop-outs and complete waste and ended up heading some of the biggest organizations; of people who went from being an average person to be a trendsetter for the entire world. IIT or its impact – if at all – was sounding too minuscule to even discuss at this platform. The question we started with was left far behind in the discussion.

'Is it really that simple to earn money?' asked Saba.

'I didn't say it is simple. I said you can earn it if you want to. It depends on how badly you want it.'

'So anyone who keeps trying eventually gets it,' replied Saba.

'Undoubtedly!!'

'In fact it can be represented in simple mathematical equations. Have you guys heard of Newton's laws of motion?'

'Nandini you are talking to engineers,' said Bharti casually.

'Oh Yes. I am sorry Newton's laws must be like your bread and butter then. Mr. Newton gave a few very interesting laws to explain the motion of bodies that can easily be extended to explain the movement of our lives.'

Already at its pinnacle our attentiveness climbed up to new heights.

'So what does the first law says?'

'Every Body will persist in its state of rest or of uniform motion (constant velocity) in a straight line unless it is compelled to change that state by forces impressed on it.'

'In context of our lives – We all continue to stay in our comfort zone until acted upon by external driving forces.'

'What sort of forces?' asked Aditya.

'These driving forces vary from person to person. They can be peer pressure, necessity, desire or sheer will power.'

That was quite impressive.

'Second law says – *Force = mass * acceleration.* For any Body of constant mass stronger the force higher is the acceleration'

'In context of our life – Driving force = K * success. K is a constant, which varies from person to person. You can imagine it as an individual's intellect, mental or physical capacity etc. Higher is the driving force, higher is the amount of effort and therefore higher success.'

It seemed the goddess of analogy herself was sitting in Nandini's form. We all kept listening mum.

'Third law – Now this one is a little tricky. *For every action there is an equal and opposite reaction.*'

'Once you start putting that hard work, which we can call action here, to achieve your goal, there is a force acting opposite which tries to stop you. This force can be of: Dejection due to lack of visible results; Depression due to some early failure; Demotivation due to lack of support; or any other 'D' natured negative noun.'

'So how do we counter this opposite force?' asked the most attentive listener, Aditya.

'Good question! Does anyone want to take this one?'

She paused for a moment but when none volunteered, she continued, 'this is where persistence comes into picture.'

'You might get dejected by lack of results or your motivation can plunge due to lack of support, you might even get depressed by some early setbacks; but persistence keeps you going and if you successfully pull through this difficult phase then there is no looking back.'

Newton might have formulated these laws but for me Nandini gave them their real purpose. I have never been more impressed by any mortal soul.

Every word out of Nandini's mouth was adding new substance to our thought streams. In fact it was creating a whirlpool of brand new set of thoughts.

The discussions went on for some more time. Bharti and Nandini explained things and cited a few more examples. Shweta and Aditya asked some questions but the rest of us were mostly listening.

We moved out of Bharti's room after a good 2 hours at around 7:00 pm.

The same black Santro and the same Kinetic Honda again traversed the corridors of the same Taj Hotel with the same set of people. But something had changed.

20

AFTER 3 YEARS

Always bear in mind that your own resolution to success is more important than any other one thing.

–Abraham Lincoln

A champion is someone who gets up, even when he can't.

–Jack Dempsey

'Honey we are getting late. Why can't you push this last five minutes of superfluous and totally redundant makeup programme a little ahead so that we can hit the office on time? Vibhor is going to kick me out.'

'Ya…..Yaah….Right! But you know what…. I think it's still better than your *'Ohh I forgot my laptop…please rush back quickly please please!!'* came the retort overflowing with vengeance.

'That happened just once!'

'Did it?'

'Okie twice…That's it'

'What about *'my mobile…left my mobile'*. Any other walking soul would have found the imitation hilarious at the least.

'Okie…okie.. fine! Now shut up and make it fast.'

'You shut up and go to hell.'

Silence prevailed for a few seconds.

'Alright...I am sorry. Honey! I am really sorry. Actually just a bit stressed because of this presentation.'

'I am sorry too.' Only the eye witnesses could believe that this voice was of the same woman who was just now screaming at her husband.

Zoooooommmm…….. started off the Black Honda Accord with the beautiful couple settled in the comfortable rear seats.

'You know what I think the lipstick is a little overdone.'

'Really...let me check.' Before she could open her makeup mirror he stopped her and said with a flirting smile, 'but I think it looks even better.' This had to be the climax of the scene as there was a chauffeur with a rear view mirror in front of him.

'Shut up!...Hey we have to be there before 7:00 pm or we are in trouble. Saba is going to kill us.'

'I cannot agree more. Presentation should be over by 6:00 pm and then I will rush. In the meantime you can go and look for a decent gift.'

'I have already got one.'

'What'

'I don't know whether you are going to like it or not. You can see it in the evening.'

21

THE WEDDING

Success seems to be largely a matter of hanging on after others have let go.

–William Feather

Thirteen virtues necessary for true success: temperance, silence, order, resolution, frugality, industry, sincerity, justice, moderation, cleanliness, tranquility, chastity, and humility.

–Benjamin Franklin

Saba was sitting on the stage with her husband – the wedding reception party had just started; and the guests were pouring in like raindrops.

I was decked in black three-piece and Samir was wearing a blue embroidered kurta with matching pajamas; we both were busy managing the party. Dad being active with the NGOs, there were quite a few celebrities making guest-appearances every now and then.

Special people need special attention, which makes them not so special, especially to the people attending them. But some are really special and so was the Lucknow City Commissioner – himself an IITian and IAS topper – who entered the gate along with two policemen and two suited gentlemen. I had met him before also and he had always been like a spiritual mentor to me. Not only to me but also for my father and hundreds and thousands of other people who have been touched by his NGO, focussed on spreading the power of positive thinking and positive attitude so as to make this world a better place to live in. As I was talking to him, my 10 year old cousin came running over to me, handed me a rolled parchment and gestured towards Saba. The scribbling read 'WHERE ARE THEY, COME HERE RIGHT NOW'.

Helplessness and frustration of a bride – unable to move freely in her reception – were clearly visible in the words. The tone also hinted that the situation was not very healthy for me as well. I rushed to the podium at the first opportunity, but not before 5-6 minutes. She was wearing a beautiful red lehnga crafted with beads and stones and was adorned in the maximum possible amount of metal, which happened to be gold – white gold (Saba hates golden gold as its way too conventional) – in this case. To complete the irritation regime was the regular standing and sitting work-out as and when some over-enthusiastic, snap thirsty, self-obsessed and self-declared photogenic freaks – as described by Saba – went up to the stage to greet the couple. Annoyance was natural, especially when it comes to our utmost idiosyncratic, unconventional and totally bohemian Saba. Pie on her perfect cake of consummate vexation was her own forced but perpetual smile which is imperative as per the norms of the society.

As I managed to reach her she said, 'Where the hell were you?' with that perpetual smile on her face.

'I was busy with the commissioner Chotu. Papa asked me to take good ....'

'Never mind. Where the hell is she?' She interrupted me in between and asked.

'She should be here any moment. Samir called her a few minutes back. She had left the airport.'

'And is Aditya coming along?'

'Umm...I don't know....actually Samir didn't ask,' I stammered.

'And what happened to those two morons. I will sue A&P if they miss the reception.'

'Chotu relax they are on their way. Actually Akshat told me he had an important presentation today.'

'Let him go to hell with his presentation. Why is Shweta not here yet?'

Shweta and Akshat got married last year. Akshat is still working with A&P whereas Shweta has joined another top consulting firm. Shweta also had an admission offer from IIM Ahmedabad which she casually rejected as she considers MBA as more of wastage of time than being anything else. She has been a fastest mover in her company and now interviews IIM graduates on the day-zero of placements for the entry level position in her firm.

'Bhaiya, call her right now.'

I said Ok and started moving away from the stage before she pulled the end of my coat.

'No..do it from here.'

'Okie okie..relax..I am calling her.'

Before I took out my cell to call her, Shweta and Akshat entered the party. They were carrying a very huge gift, which was somehow balanced in two sets of arms. After carefully settling the gift on a table Shweta rushed to greet Saba.

'Hi di...Sorry I am late...but you know who to be blamed...Ohh you look amazing.'

In any normal conversation for all the above fragmented sentences the speaker would expect a reply. But here the speaker was perhaps not interested in one and the listener was seemingly fine by it. This is probably among the normal practices of their cult.

'Thanks,' came out the reply finally.

'Yaar Anjali has still not arrived. She is bringing my footwear, I ordered through internet.'

'Ohh that golden one with beads on it and very high heels,' came out the excited reply.

'Yeah...Yeah,' came out the even more excited one.

'She is an idiot I told her to take an early flight. She had some important conference in London.'

Anjali has completed her third year and is doing her internship in Columbia University, New York, USA in Genetic Algorithm which by the way is a subfield or should say the core of Artificial Intelligence. It is a fully paid internship and she is also getting this 4 days fly-back to attend the marriage.

Shweta spent good fifteen minutes on the stage and then as she was coming down to meet my parents and other family members Anjali came rushing in with a huge polythene bag in her hand. She was togged in blue jeans, dark red sweat shirt and a denim jacket and was definitely coming straight from the airport. The exertion of the 8 hours London – New Delhi flight was apparent from her face but it was miserably inadequate to take away the charm.

She straight away went to Saba up on the stage with the huge packet. In a sudden occurrence of multiple events quite a few of bride's friends went up on to the stage to get their snap clicked and in this process somehow hid the bride completely from the eyes of the guests. In a few seconds the bride reappeared and the snap was clicked. Although everything happened in a flash but I couldn't help but notice. Saba noticed that I noticed and pointed at her feet. She had changed her sandals. Wow!

'Di..I am sorry I got late,' said Anjali.

'You were just on time.'

'Where is that bugger Aditya?' asked Saba.

'Di, he couldn't make it as his group has taken part in the robotics competition. He is extremely busy with that. He will be back for a week after 20th June.'

Aditya was also doing his intern in the same university in the mechanical engineering department.

'Anju, take the key of room number 309 from mummy. Your stuff is there. Go and get ready.' Shweta commanded her baby sister and she followed obediently as always.

'Sahil Bhai…Sahil bhai.' Danish, my cousin, came running to me. 'Her Majesty just entered the gates of the Palace.'

Danish is more of a friend than a cousin. He is just two years younger to me and has always been my secret keeper. He came to tell that Sarah's family had arrived. Sarah was my fiancée.

Sarah was doing her graduation in English, was a traditional Muslim girl and was beautiful beyond imagination. She was attired in a pink salwar-suit with perfectly matching jewelry. She was looking AWESOME. In the 45 minutes of her stay I could not dare to even look at her properly, let aside talking. The only moment we came a little closer was when her family went up to the stage to greet the couple and Saba forcefully dragged me in for the snap and craftily made me stand right next to her.

The party went pretty well and by 12:30 am only family and close friends were left. Saba was finally able to come down from the podium. While her husband was busy attending few of his closest friends, Saba settled on the table specially decorated for the bride and the groom. Samir, Yash and I joined her. Saba called Shweta and Anjali too. Akshat had already left for his place as Shweta had plans to stay with her family today. Now it was just the six of us sitting at that table.

I don't know what were the others thinking but I couldn't help but remember the similar scene three years back when all of us – all including Aditya – were sitting together in my living room. There were just a few differences here: instead of a living room in a government apartment in Lucknow we were in a five-star hotel lawn in Delhi; instead of a few sad faces trying to console few other dejected ones everybody was vibrant and happy; instead of a shy and nervous Anjali there was a blue lehnga-clad, jewelry-loaded, Ivy-League intern student, beaming Anjali; instead of a frustrated and dismayed Shweta there was a superbly successful corporate executive flashing her charm in her exorbitantly expensive attire.

As I came out of this nostalgia I thought I missed out on some conversation just to find out that nobody was speaking anything. Everyone was perhaps going through the same analysis in their own perspective. Silence seemed to be the choice and it prevailed undisturbed until Saba's cell phone rang.

'Hello'

'Hi di. Congratulations.'

'ADITYA'

'Yeah.'

'You useless bugger!!! Moron!! Where the hell are you?'

'I am sorry I could not come as there is a very important contest on....'

'Shut up and go to hell...'

'I am really sorry. Will definitely make it up to you di.'

'Shut up.'

'Sorry.'

'Shut up. By the way the watch you gifted her is going pretty well with her blue lehnga.'

It was not very challenging to predict the expressions of the watch giver but the recipient was definitely crimsoned and the rest of us were grinning.

> To laugh often and much, to win the respect of intelligent people and the affection of children, to earn the appreciation of honest critics and endure the betrayal of false friends, to appreciate beauty, to find the best in others, to leave the world a bit better, whether by a healthy child, a garden patch, or a redeemed social condition; to know even one life has breathed easier because you have lived. This is to have succeeded!
>
> ~Ralph Waldo Emerson

Through these 36000+ words all I have tried to convey is that failures are an integral part of our life and there is no success without failure. Our failures help us to learn; they should inspire us and should be a source of our motivation; as they were for some of the greatest people ever.